D0927948

THE JAYHAWKERS

Every cattle drive that left Texas met with disaster. Men were killed, herds disappeared, and the few survivors who made it back home were broken and penniless. It was the work of the Jayhawkers: everyone knew, but no one could stop it.

One Texas cattleman refused to be beaten. His name was Mike Gould, and after losing his own herd, he signed on with a drive that was headed straight for Jayhawker territory. His boss was a high-spirited feline beauty who didn't know the dangers he faced. But Mike knew.

Sooner or later, the marauding Jayhawkers would attack and he would be ready for them. Ready with plans that would mean the end of the Jayhawkers' reign . . . or the end of Go-to-hell Gould.

THE JAYHAWKERS

L. L. Foreman

GUNSMOKE

FOR

This hardback edition 2006
by BBC Audiobooks Ltd
by arrangement with
Golden West Literary Agency

ISBN 1 4056 8076 8

British Library Cataloguing in Publication Data available.

Printed and bound in Great Britain by
Antony Rowe Ltd., Chippenham, Wiltshire

CHAPTER ONE

Down on Lost Creek, in Goliad County, Texas, nobody got rich in the cattle business. It was a community of cowmen-settlers who shared the open range, pitched in together at roundup time, sold off their beeves where they could, and hoped for better prices next year. They made out.

They humped along until what became known as "The Byler Bust" cost them their beef crop and broke them flat.

Being cowmen, and therefore desperately optimistic as well as single-minded, they held a cow hunt to see what they could comb out of the brush—stuff that had escaped the spring roundup and maybe several before that—and added to it the majority of their remaining stock, closely calculating the maximum they could afford to sell. The agreement was to shape up the whole gather into a single trail herd and point it north. They looked to one Mike Gould to boss the drive, handle the selling end, and make them once again solvent. Mike Gould owned eight hundred head that he intended taking up the trail, anyway, and they felt he could just as well take theirs along with his. A neighborly act, though he didn't neighbor with anybody much.

A run of misfortunes, large and small, plagued the outfit before it got started. Tempers crackled. They were road-branding grown steers, many of them old brush outlaws, the scrapings of the range. The steers objected strenuously to ropes and men and hot irons. There wasn't a man on the crew who hadn't lost some skin, rope-burned his fingers, or picked up a limp.

Mike Gould had reached the point of growling at everybody, including the cowmen who owned shares with him in the herd. He was halfway wishing that he hadn't taken on to make the drive. His eight hundred head could have been well on the trail by now, with a small crew and no problems that weren't entirely his own. Better to have kept himself free and unencumbered, a loner. *He travels the fastest who travels alone.* A man who let in partners was letting in grief.

"When d'you reckon you'll get up to Kansas?" Old Man Burris asked. He owned thirty head of the herd. Mike didn't reply. Fool question. Flooded rivers, dry stretches, summer storms—a time schedule? Kansas grangers up in arms against Texas cattle. Have to scout out a lonely spot to cross.

The spare wagon, returning from Peck's Store with a load of supplies, came rattling right through the busy branding ground at near runaway speed. Its driver was the camp cook, a Dutchman who sometimes forgot that the half-wild long-horns weren't the placid Holsteins of his native land. True to the hoodoo, a big brute of a steer took advantage of the distraction to break loose from its captors, scattering men and hot irons.

Some of the crew chuckled, gleaning wry comedy from the mishap, but Mike Gould shouted angrily after the cook, "Goddam knothead, rompsing through camp like a drunk Tonk!"

Eb Saunders, owner of a hundred and sixty head, said to him, "You've sure got hell in your neck these days, Mike! Ease up, why don't you?"

Others in the group of partners nodded, and Old Man Burris complained, "Can't hardly get a civil word out of him today. No call to act so wringy. Not to us, anyhow."

Mike Gould, about to ride after the wagon, swung back to them. Hard irritation straightened his wide mouth. His dark gray eyes, lightened to opaque slate by the contrast of deeply browned skin, played over them.

"Gentlemen," he said, bitingly polite, "maybe you'll recall we all agreed I'd have three thousand head to put on the trail. I took on a crew for that size herd. I gathered horses and got fixed for supplies accordingly, on my pocket and my credit. What happens? Eleven hundred head short—sold out! Damn right I'm wringy!"

Joel Rupe, called Parson by reason of a mild disposition, said, "Let's don't cuss Choate and the others too much for selling their cows to Cullen. They needed ready cash, bad." He squinted down at the empty pipe in his teeth. "O' course, we all do, since Byler's Bust. But they was hurt the hardest. Henry Bell, for one, I know for a fact his kids was eating jackrabbit. And him a colonel once!"

"I respect your charitable outlook, Parson," Mike Gould told him, small respect in his tone. "But I'm left with more men and horses than I can use or pay for. I've got to cut down, way down. I've got a lot a figuring to do. I'll be off to a late start as it is, and here you come pestering me with questions. Dammit, don't cry for any guarantees I'll get your cows up to market! I'll do my best, that's all I promise!"

"Nobody's asking for any guarantees. We—"

"Then quit dealing me misery!" Mike's frayed temper snapped. "You want a civil word? Me up to my neck in work? Go to hell!"

"Those ain't civil words," Eb Saunders observed acidly, "but they're sure in character, Mr. Go-to-hell Gould!"

"Guess we're just rightly anxious, is all," put in one of the men.

"Don't pour it on me. Save it till I'm on my way north." Mike paused, reminding himself that these were his neighbors, partners in the herd. He owned more cattle in the herd than any three of them, but their worries were heavier than his. They had families to feed. He had only himself to worry about.

"Look," he said, less harshly, "it's okay if you vote to back out. Cullen's still buying, far's I know. He seems to have all the money in the world."

Harley Cullen had lately come down into Goliad County to buy Texas cattle cheap, for a herd that he was gathering to drive north. He wasn't a Texan, nor did he bear the marks of a cattleman, but he knew how and when to rig a bargain. Six dollars a head was his standing offer, yet he found small ranchers hard-pressed for ready cash who would sell to him, grudgingly, hating to do it. Five of Mike's neighbors had done so, shamedly pulling out of their agreement and throwing Mike's calculations out of kilter.

The Cullen camp lay only a short mile farther down Lost Creek, a comfortable outfit of tents and wagons under a stand of cottonwoods. An affront to Mike's ears was the bawling of Cullen's increasing herd.

"Would you sell yours to Cullen at his price?" Eb Saunders asked Mike.

"Hell, no! They'll fetch forty a head up north."

"*If* you can get 'em there. Byler didn't."

They had all, except Mike Gould, lost heavily on Byler in the spring, leaving them not only broke but in debt for their last winter's bills. Byler was an experienced stockman and drover, and the Lost Creek cowmen had readily turned their beefs over to him, for him to sell for them on commission up north. That was his business and he was famed for getting the best price. The beef market was soaring, and they dreamed of new boots, new saddles, and dress goods for the womenfolks.

But up in the Indian Territory, Byler lost the whole herd, his own horses, three of his riders—one his cousin—and struggled back home a sick man.

"Byler's ain't the only trail outfit that gone to smash this year," Joel Rupe mentioned. "Man from over Wilson County was telling me—"

"There's risk," Mike Gould granted impatiently. "There gen'rally is, where there's high profit. Up north they're hollering for beef, we know that. They had that big freeze-up last winter. Now there's this quarantine thing, this deadline that the Kansas grangers are trying to slap against Texas cows."

"Trying?" Old Man Burris said sardonically. "Ask Byler how they're trying!"

"I've talked to him. He wasn't busted by any Kansas grangers scared of fever ticks." Mike thought of that capable stockman's haunted eyes. "It was a pack of goddam Jayhawkers. They jumped him before he ever got in sight of Kansas. They made out like they were grangers, but there's a big difference."

"What difference?"

"Grangers don't gen'rally go to murder in cold blood, for one thing. Jayhawkers do. These did."

Joel Rupe said, "That man from over Wilson County was telling me they'll stompede a herd and kill any man they catch with it. They hold a mock trial and flog him dead."

Old Man Burris hunched his narrow shoulders uneasily. "That's another risk, a bad one!" He peered around at the solemn faces, before asking Mike, "Is it a fact they're damn-Yankees?"

"Jayhawkers?" Mike shrugged. "Call 'em anything. Soldiers mustered out of the Yankee army. Deserters. Rustlers, renegades, outlaws from all over, hiding in the Indian Territory. Take your pick, they've got 'em. They all claim they're Kansans, protecting Kansas from fever ticks spreading up from Texas, but that's just a damn lie to keep the real Kansas grangers on their side. They raid the herds and smuggle 'em up themselves."

"How 'bout the ticks?"

"Come cold weather, our fever ticks don't flourish up north. Can't convince those grangers of it, though. They're scared for their own cows, and they think every Texas cow carries the fever."

Yearly, settlers' anxieties about the Texas fever had created trouble along the northern trails. Texas cattle were immune to it, but they carried the ticks, and in summer the cattle farther north were apt to pick them up and fall victim to the splenetic fever. The danger had been inflated beyond its actuality, for the ticks didn't infest all Texas cattle, and a northern winter usually ended it; but a settler in a panic over his dozen cows wasn't likely to listen to reason from a big-hatted Texan wanting to cross a herd of longhorns over his land.

"I guess," said Old Man Burris, "you *sabe* how things lay up there."

"I've been there a time or two, years I wasn't here," Mike answered sparely.

The talk threatened to drift out of bounds, so he steered it back with a blunt statement of his position. "I'm making this drive, as I planned to do since long before you fellows put in with Byler. Anybody wants to cut out, say so right now. My cows are going up with me, regardless."

Why, he wondered, did he concern himself on their account? He supposed the answer lay in his feeling about poverty being a bad neighbor. He was out to make something of himself in a hurry, and penniless neighbors were a liability. All he owned so far was his herd of steers, gained by hard work, a lot of doing-without, and some gambling, but the payoff promised to run better than thirty thousand dollars—a long step forward to make up for years squandered in the past.

Eb Saunders said presently, after a silent conference of looks and nods, "Our cows stay in the herd, Mike, as agreed. We'll gamble on you to—"

"That's settled, then," Mike cut him off, and rode on after the wagon.

They watched him cut across the branding ground through the dust and moil of bawling steers, darting riders, flying ropes, and sweating men working with hot irons. "Hell in his neck is right!" Old Man Burris commented. "Don't he ever laugh, Parson?"

Joel Rupe thought about it. "I've seen him kinda smile."

"Musta hurt him!"

"What's to laugh about?" one of the others, himself a mirthless man, inquired. "Ain't nothing funny in shaping up a trail herd, outfitting it on a shoestring and a dab of credit. Me, for a hard job I'll take a hard man."

"You've got one," Eb Saunders said. He spat over his horse's head. "No, he don't laugh."

"You knew him when he was a kid, didn't you, Eb? Before he went off?"

"We was kids together. That was when he done all his laughing. So did I. Before we knew how poor we were."

"And now you're poor again."

"I am. Not him. He's betting all he's got on this drive, and he'll make it or die. I mean that. He can't stand to lose."

CHAPTER TWO

The cook's helper for the day, Mig Apodaca, already was stripping the harness off the wagon team. In the wagon lay only a sack of flour, and Mike said to him, "You unloaded fast, Mig."

Bruno Polzer, the cook, looked up from cleavering dinner beef on the tail of the chuck wagon alongside. They had killed and butchered a steer that broke its leg—another mishap. He was short and round, of a more cheerful disposition than most cooks until something upset him, when he tended to bang things around and curse everybody in Dutch.

"Ain't unload nutting," he told Mike. "One sack flour all I brung from Peck's."

Mike held back an exasperated blast. "How about the bacon and coffee, and all the rest of the stuff I ordered?"

"Cullen!" Bruno brandished the cleaver. "Cullen! He wass buying all Peck got! Sonna-bitch pay cash!"

"What? Peck said he'd let me have all we need. You must've got it twisted. He knows one sack of flour's no good to us."

"Hah!" The cleaver whammed. "You go tell Peck!"

"I'm about to do that." Mike turned his horse and rode off out of camp, scowling.

Peck's Store, the only store on Lost Creek, carried only bare necessities and no great quantity of those. Its owner, a worried little man of frugal ways, shrank from stocking up too far ahead and in consequence he frequently ran short. Byler's disaster had hit him, too—the cowmen's yearlong bills went hung up and caught him in the pinch.

A lanky cowhand using a baling hook was loading a large

and well-filled wagon out front, watched by Harley Cullen
and the pleased storekeeper. Behind the wagon stood a light
buckboard, black and neat, its team a smart little pair of
brown ponies. Cullen glanced in Mike's direction as he rode
up, but gave no sign of recognition. Mike dismounted and
tied his horse. Peck's pleased expression faded.

"That's everything, Peel," Cullen said to the cowhand. He
called into the store, "Ready, Joyce?"

He was a heavily built man of middle age, with some
gray in his square-cut beard. Wearing a black coat and neck-
tie despite the day's heat, and a flat-brimmed hat set straight
on his large head, he resembled a solid Mormon elder, a
prosperous farmer, a country banker, anything but a cattleman.

Mike confronted Peck. He had never met Harley Cullen,
though he knew him by sight only too well, having seen him
driving about in his buckboard on cattle-buying jaunts. He
said curtly to Peck, "You sent my cook back with a sack of
flour." He stuck a thumb at the loaded wagon. "That my stuff?"

The little storekeeper shook his head. "S-sorry," he stammered. "That's Mr. Cullen's. The s-sack of flour was all I
could s-spare you."

"I spoke for the stuff a week ago!" Mike snapped.

"No, no, you—you misunderstood. I meant your credit
was good for—for anything I had in stock when you sent
for it."

"That's a damn lie!"

"Mr. Gould!" Peck quavered. "I'm a respectable—"

"You've sold out from under me! To a Yankee, at that!"

"Now see here!" Cullen interposed. He had the direct gaze
and manner of a man who was accustomed to wielding
authority. "Mr. Peck has every right to sell his goods to who-
ever—"

"I'll get to you later," Mike said. "It's him I'm talking
to now." He asked Peck, "What's left in the store?"

"Nothing you could use, I'm afraid," Peck answered nervously. He spread his hands. "Look, try to understand. I'm
having to carry a stack of unpaid bills. Money's scarce, you
know that. A cash customer comes first—has to, if I'm to
stay in business."

Mike slapped his thigh in frustration. Here it was again,
the same bitter necessity that had forced Choate and the
others to sell their cows to Cullen at a robbery price. The
pressure of poverty. The mean shifts and expedients, on down

to breaking agreements, twisting one's own words, and weaseling out of promises.

"All right, Peck," he sighed. "I'll try to see it your way, but I don't take to it. You've put me in a corner."

A sharp dig in his shoulder spun him around. The point of the baling hook pierced his shirt, and Cullen's lanky cowhand drawled. "How 'bout picking somebody more your size, Texan?"

Mike said promptly, "You'll do!" He batted him backhand in the mouth, glad to vent his feelings. The baling hook caught in the shoulder seam and ripped his sleeve off.

The man came at him, bright-eyed and eager, ignoring a quick command from Cullen to hold off. Cullen had brought a crew down to Lost Creek, men from up beyond Baxter Springs, none of them Texans. They were an uncommonly tough-looking bunch, hired for their ability to protect the herd on the trail. Cullen had been heard to state flatly that the trouble with Texas trail outfits came from picking crews more for their knowledge of cattle than of battle. His battlers would finish the drive, where other outfits, possibly more cattle-wise, would come to grief.

This tough battler didn't belie his looks. His left fist rammed Mike back on his heels, and he brought the baling hook slashing up in his right hand for a swift finish. Mike pulled in his head and dodged the point, but the round of the steel hook fetched him a crack on the chin that toppled him back another step.

Peck bleated, "No, no! Mr. Cullen—!"

Mike kicked out. The heel of his boot caught the man in the knee, in mid-stride. He heard his hiss, saw the hook waver an instant in its circling stroke, and he stroked out his gun.

"Drop that thing!"

The man lowered it, looking down at it regretfully, slowly raising his fingers one by one from the wooden handle. He had set his mind on using it, a rare weapon, something to talk about, and hated to let it go. Dangling it between two fingers, he cut a sly look upward at Mike's eyes to calculate the degree of his alertness. Mike struck fast at it with the barrel of his gun. The hook bounced on the ground. The man jerked back his empty hand. Mike holstered his gun, easing down the cocked hammer.

"Now we'll start over."

He hit him a ringing clout on the ear with the open palm

of his hand. The man reeled, blinking, then a rage of indignation at the insulting nature of the blow brought him plunging forward, fists swinging. Mike let him close in, taking punishment, dug twice at his stomach, and jolted him with a straight-arm slam in the chest. The swinging fists spread wide for balance. Again his open palm slapped like a pistol shot, and next his other hand made impact, full across the face. He was holding it against the man for trying to skewer him with the baling hook. To beat him up for it was not enough. He would belittle and humble him as well.

Half blinded, the cowhand rushed at him. In his injured pride he cast aside caution and tricks, and another fearful whack in the face maddened him into clawing at his gun. Mike fetched him a final belt, grabbed his gun-arm and slung him around, and booted him in the seat of his pants. The wagon team shied as he took a header.

Cullen hurried to hold the horses. He sent Mike a chill stare. "Did you have to do that to him?"

"I did," Mike said. He picked up his hat. "And I could wish it'd been you, if you'd been younger!"

"You brute!" said a girl standing in the store doorway.

She was young and more than pretty, a fair-haired girl with eyes oddly like Mike's own, dark gray. Her prettiness and her eyes failed to win Mike's favor. He knew her, as he did Cullen, only by sight. She was Cullen's niece, a circumstance that Mike viewed as regrettable and certainly not calculated to endear her to him. He had wondered once or twice at the situation—a girl in a cow camp. Maybe she was no better than she ought to be. Maybe the niece-uncle thing was just a convenient arrangement. She didn't a bit resemble Harley Cullen.

"Speaking to me?" he inquired.

"Yes!" She stepped out from the doorway. Her blue dress shimmered in the sun. "Are all Texans like you?"

He shook his head. "We run to several breeds."

"I'm glad to hear it. You—you're an animal!"

"You're a lady," he returned. He let a moment go by, and added ungently, "Maybe we're both wrong."

Cullen had helped his cowhand onto the loaded wagon, but seeing that the man wasn't in shape to drive it, he climbed up and himself took the lines. "Let's get away from here, Joyce!" he said to the girl.

Passing Mike, she drew her skirts aside and wrinkled her nose. He had been working right along with his crew, hadn't shaved for days, and was stinking dirty. Still, her deliberate display of revulsion galled him. Everybody knew what cow folks hard at work looked like. She was staying in a cow camp, herself, even if she did look as fresh as bluebonnets after a rain.

On impulse, he trod lightly after her to the buckboard. As she picked up her skirts to climb up, he slid his hands under her armpits and lifted her. The softness under his hands instantly tightened, but she didn't struggle, didn't utter a sound. She composed herself on the seat after he released her, straightened out her skirts, and picked up the lines. She plucked the whip from its socket and unwound the leash, gazing ahead.

The whip whistled. The sting of it on his neck and back so surprised him that he jumped, hung a spur on the edge of Peck's skimpy boardwalk, and sat down hard. Wheels spun, and the trim rig pulled away, the girl still gazing ahead.

When Mike got back to camp, Eb Saunders walked all around him inspecting his damages, and asked, "What did you get into?"

"Tangled with one of Cullen's crew," Mike said briefly. He fingered the welt on his neck. "And that girl of his."

"His niece?"

"If that's what she is. How's work coming?"

"Juan says they're about winding it up. Says maybe you could start out tomorrow."

"Should. Late start as it is. The boys'll have to go it on beef and biscuits for a while. Cullen cleaned Peck out."

Eb Saunders put his hands to his head. "Holy Moses, what next! Ain't it hell being poor?"

Mike nodded. "I'll pick up supplies at Lockhart. Coffee and bacon, anyhow. I can sell off some of the extra horses there and along the route. We'll make out."

"You're taking on a tough load, Mike. Don't think we don't appreciate it." Eb Saunders sighed, and looked away. "Wish I could make the drive with you, but you know how 'tis. Wife and kids."

"Yeah. Don't sell 'em to Cullen."

Eb shot Mike a stiff stare, then grinned. "Six dollars a head? I'd like to bust a cap at that Kansas buzzard, or whatever he is, for putting you in a fix."

"Wouldn't much mind, myself. I just hope his outfit doesn't catch up with mine on the trail, or I might do that."

Mike absently scratched his back, and winced. "Wonder what he's going to do about the girl?"

"*Qui'n sabe?* Could be he figures to take her 'long with the outfit." Eb eyed Mike curiously, seeing him shake his head scowlingly at the unlikely suggestion. "Reminds me—are you keeping Juan on as your segundo? None of my business, but, well, a Mexican—"

"Juan Bujac's a top cowhand, and he's been around. We get along. He stays on as my segundo, yeah."

"You were gone from Texas a good long time." Ed observed, "and maybe you forgot a thing or two. There's some Texans don't relish taking a Mexican's orders. Might find some in your crew."

"If so, they can go to hell," Mike said casually.

"That's one way you ain't changed. It's always been your answer to problems that ain't got an answer." Eb Saunders' slow grin came. "Go-to-hell Gould, the kid who drug me home thorugh the worst dust storm in memory, both our ponies lost and me with a busted foot. I told you to leave me or we'd both perish, and you told me to—"

"Aw, go to hell!" Mike said, and went to tell his crew the bad news about the beef and biscuits.

The Lost Creek outfit got off to its start the next day, Sunday, a day that some held was unlucky for the start of a cattle drive, the Lord intending it for more spiritual purposes. Mike Gould wanted to get well ahead of the Cullen herd, which was readying to move out. Most of the cows in both herds had been range mates; given a chance they'd mix and renew old acquaintance, creating no end of trouble. Mike had no intention of wasting a day, now or henceforth until he reached Abilene in Kansas. To objections he raised the argument that the Lord would overlook the transgression because He understood cattlemen's problems along with all lesser matters.

Despite the calamity-groaners, the drive began well, possibly because all hands half expected the worst and did their best to stave it off. They strung the herd out in a multicolored ribbon that stretched for a mile, the wrangler bringing up the remuda behind. A big steer elected itself leader and took its place at the head of the herd, while other steers found traveling partners by some system of choice known only to themselves.

For the first few days they pushed the herd along pretty

hard, getting it road-broke, after which the men and cattle alike settled down to the daily routine of the trail. Finding good grass, and grazing as they traveled, the steers began putting on flesh.

At Lockhart, Mike traded off some of the extra horses for supplies, ending the famine in the commissary department, and bought tobacco for the crew. Spirits perked up. The hoodoo that had plagued the outfit, they agreed, was left behind. It wasn't a traveler. Juan Bujac, smilingly tactful, caused no friction as Mike's segundo. He had brought along a guitar, and evenings around the cookfire he played old Texas favorites: "Cotton-Eyed Joe," "Old Dan Tucker," "Hogs In The Cornfield" . . .

"I learned them specially for this trip," he privately confided to Mike. "They are not very tuneful to my ear, but—" he shrugged "—the Mexican songs do not please Texans."

"They please me, and I'm a Texan," Mike said.

Juan smiled. They were riding ahead of the herd, scouting out a bedding ground for the night. "You have lived in other places. You know Mexico. You speak Spanish."

"Kitchen Spanish. Not hidalgo Spanish like yours."

Turning the subject instantly, Juan said, "There looks a good spot yonder. I'll ride on and look it over. My horse needs a run."

Watching him spur his horse to a run, Mike wondered about his background. He and Juan Bujac had detected at first sight a certain quality that they shared in common, something that had nothing whatever to do with the far different roots from which they had sprung. They had taken each other's measure and recognized the signs of brotherhood.

Mike turned back, relying on Juan's judgment to locate by sundown a good bedding ground for the herd. A valuable man to have along, Juan, in more ways than one. Mig Apodaca, a good *vaquero* in his own right, paid him respect.

"Couldn't ask for a better crew, much," Mike muttered to himself. The long trail ahead would put them to the test. His thoughts harked back to Cullen. Surely Cullen wasn't bringing that girl along. A cattle drive was no place for any woman. The discomforts, the difficult inconveniences, and that hardcase crew of his . . .

"Well—not my problem."

They trailed north by way of Austin, crossing the Colorado River a couple of miles below town, and on up by Round

Rock, Georgetown, Salado, Belton, to the Brazos. Crossing the Brazos to the west of Cleburne, three easy days brought the herd past Hell's Half Acre east of Fort Worth.

Beyond Fort Worth they began having trouble from horse thieves. Nothing out of the ordinary. The thieves slipped in among the horses at night and drifted a few out. Hobbling the horses did no good. A thief could the more easily catch those he wanted, cut the hobbles, and lead them away. Mike put on Randy Burr, youngest member of the crew, to night-hawk the remuda. Randy was liable to fall asleep on watch, but he was a light sleeper and his ears stayed awake. He whittled down the losses. In due course the face of the moon grew to where only a Comanche would try sneaking up unseen.

Apart from near-stampedes, soaking rainstorms, bone-dry stretches, and a bad crossing at Red River Station that cost two days' time and seven drowned steers, the drive continued uneventful.

Now in the Indian Territory, they struck the line of Nation Beaver Creek, pushed on to Rush Springs, then to the Little Washita and on to Washita Crossing, once in a while giving beef to Indians demanding it. For going on forty days they hadn't seen another trail herd. The trail drivers were shy this risky year.

Not until they were across the South Fork of the Canadian River, when the trail hands were discussing how they would spend their pay in Abilene on rich and riotous living, did the hoodoo catch up with them.

CHAPTER THREE

"Cuidado!" Juan Bujac sang out to Mike. He had been ranging forward of the moving herd, and came spurring back.

Mike, who was keeping the lead steer company, rode to meet him. It was around four o'clock in the afternoon, and the outfit was winding through a broken piece of country thick in oak and high bluestem grass.

A group of riders bore down on the herd. Most of them were bearded and shaggy-haired, looking earthy in unwashed clothes, but they rode good horses and carried a wider assortment of weapons than a raiding Comanche band after a successful summer.

"Jayhawkers!" Mike said. "Ever seen them?"

"I've seen their kind." Juan Bujac folded his hands over his reins. *"Animaluchos!"*

The leading rider threw up his hand, and the others straggled to a halt behind him. In place of a hat he wore a blue bandanna tied around his head. He carried two belted guns and a knife, a carbine in fringed buckskin saddle scabbard, and a heavy double-barreled shotgun.

"This herd don't go no fu'ther!" he declared with blaring arrogance and no preliminaries. "You're all under arrest!"

"What's your authority?" Mike asked him, knowing in advance the answer.

"We're protectin' Kansas from your goddam Texas fever ticks!"

"We're still in the Indian Territory. Kansas authority doesn't reach down here—nor any other but federal." Mike shaded his tone to that of a troubled man offering a reasonable argument. He watched the group of men exchange sardonic grins, slouching in their saddles, relaxed in the expectation of an easy coup.

"Take 'em, boys!" The leader lifted his shotgun to blast into the oncoming herd and stampede it.

Mike drew and fired in a heartbeat. Beside him, Juan Bujac abruptly quit his horse, shooting before his feet touched the ground, a gun in each hand. He wore only a single holster. Where he kept his holdout gun only he knew.

In the chattering roar of gunfire the lounging Jayhawkers became a shattered tangle of shocked men fighting their rearing horses, colliding, triggering wild shots. Their leader was down, twice hit, one foot caught in a stirrup and his body wrenched about by his panicked horse. A man howled curses, clinging to his saddlehorn until bucked off. Another bowed low and cried out for help, but the rest were too busy and let him tumble.

Swapping his emptied gun for his rifle, Mike snapped off three shots before he had to grab the reins of his plunging horse. Juan Bujac was coolly advancing through his own smoke, a pistolero picking his targets. Some of the trail crew, those on point and forward sideline, came tearing along the column of cattle.

The Jayhawkers scattered, yelling threats, and Juan Bujac turned and walked back. The short and savage fight hadn't ruffled him. "We got four," he reported to Mike, "and damaged some others."

Mike rode after his horse, caught it, and brought it to him. "Knew I could rely on you," he said.

Their eyes met. Juan smiled. "Knew I was in reliable company."

"Jeez!" exclaimed a trail hand, staring down at the dead men. "What'll we do with 'em?"

"Drag 'em off the trail," Mike ordered. "No time to bury 'em." The herd was piling up, and he called, "String out— string those cows out and keep moving! Juan, stay on scout. We'll make a moonlight drive tonight and lay up somewhere tomorrow."

He rode down one side of the trail herd to the drag, remuda, and chuck wagon, and up the other side, telling the riders of his decision. He met some predictable grumblings.

"What, no supper?"

"Grab cold meat and biscuits from the chuck wagon and eat in the saddle!"

"A night drive's no joke!"

"Neither's a stampede and a bullet for breakfast! The gang we busted's only a sample. They'll spread the word. Sooner we reach Abilene the better. We're noways safe till then, so stay awake!"

"Is it all right to shut one eye?"

"No! You can sleep tomorrow, when we locate a right spot to hole up. Hot grub and coffee then, too."

"How d'you hide nineteen hundred cows?"

"It's a big country. We'll do what we can."

They kept the herd on the move all through the night, weary and disgruntled cows bawling complaints, the drag riders falling far behind with the loafers. Near sunup Mike and Juan located a hill-sheltered spot well off the trail, and guided the leaders to it. It took time to bring the whole herd up and get it bedded down, and the sun was two hours high before the chuck wagon rolled in, the cook cussing in Dutch. They had entered a dry stretch of country during the night, and the cook had somehow managed to lose his way in the heavy pall of kicked-up dust.

By then the men were stone asleep, too worn out to think of eating. Mike and Juan took on the first guard, and talked things over when they met on their rounds, circling the herd. With some humor, Juan remarked that a trail boss and his segundo were not usually expected to carry the load with the crew.

Mike shrugged. "Who'd do it if we didn't? These Lost Creek boys are a long way from home, but on the whole it's gone easy up to now. Twenty-four hours in the saddle did 'em in. Let 'em sleep. We can catch up on ours later."

Juan shook his head. "I have done without sleep before. And you, I think."

"Many a time." Again their glances touched. Mike said, "We better make an early start this evening, so's to cross North Fork while it's still light."

"Do you believe this night-driving will put the Jayhawkers off our tracks?"

"Let's say it's the best idea I can come up with. They're less apt to catch us at night. By day, in a place like this, all hands on tap, we're as ready for 'em as we can ever be."

"It is a good idea," Juan conceded, "but I wish we were closer to Kansas. Another night or two, and they'll know what we're doing. Then what?"

"Tomorrow I'll see what else I can think of."

"Not of turning back, of course," Juan murmured.

Mike looked at him. "After coming this far? Hell! Let's go shake awake the next watch. Bruno'll have something cooking by this time, if he's still on his feet."

The herd made the North Fork crossing before sundown with no more than an ordinary amount of trouble, and headed on up north, steers sniffing and bellowing for mislaid traveling partners, riders hastily wringing out their clothes.

On the north bank Bruno Polzer staged a one-man mutiny, flatly refusing to drive the chuck wagon behind the drag and remuda. Never again. The country ahead looked to be fairly grassed, not dry, but nothing could convince the cook that tonight wouldn't be a repetition of last night's dust. He'd had his fill of it, and also he intimated that trundling at the tail end of the herd was unbefitting to his dignity and position. He disliked the smell of cow droppings, too. If he couldn't travel apart from the herd, preferably up front in fresh air, then he would quit. Where in the Territory he would quit to, he didn't clarify, but he was Dutch-stubborn enough to walk off, so Mike let him have his way.

Juan Bujac mentioned that he had known of trail outfits that regularly followed their chuck wagon, one advantage being that the cook, arriving first on the bedding ground, could be getting a meal ready for the men when they rounded in.

Mike nodded. "I know. Only thing is, Bruno lets his team out when nothing stops him. He's liable to drive on too far ahead, and he's a genius at losing himself."

The section of trail they were following had been traveled over by many herds of previous years. It had become worn down to a broad indentation in the earth, curving around wooded hills, and for stretches it was as passable as a stage road. The chuck wagon drew onward, Bruno Polzer happily clucking to his team, glorying in the freedom to choose his own gait.

There seemed scant chance that anybody, even Bruno, could go astray on this piece of trail, but around midnight Mike told Mig Apodaca to ride on after him. "Tell him to wait for us to catch up. Dammit, I haven't seen him since he took off."

Mig Apodaca was gone a long time. On his return, grinning, he reported that he had come upon the chuck wagon about three miles up the trail. Bruno had a fire started and was boiling coffee for the crew, singing at his work.

"Coffee sounds good," Mike said. "Just so he puts his fire out before the herd gets there."

Although the night-driving change of routine had caused fretful discontent in the herd, and some of the more restless steers were becoming troublesome, the outfit averaged a mile an hour. The rate was satisfactory on the whole, but Juan Bujac, coming up alongside Mike, remarked that he'd never take to trail driving as a regular thing. Too slow for him.

Mike grinned crookedly. "It can get fast in an *estampida,* so don't gripe! We're not through yet." In another hour he said, "There's Bruno's fire. Go tell him—"

He bit off the rest, staring ahead. "Hell—that's no cook-fire! Come on!"

They hit their horses forward and pulled away from the herd. As they rounded a tree-fringed curve of the trail, Juan Bujac exclaimed, *"Dulce Cristo!* The fat fool has set fire to the wagon!"

The fire was a great, glowing mass that brightened when a breeze touched it, small flames flickering, then dulling again to angry red. Their horses balked, fearing to go nearer. They left them ground-reined and went forward on foot.

And there go all our supplies, Mike thought, before he raised his eyes and saw what he knew must be Bruno Polzer. The team was gone. The wagon had been rolled under an oak tree beside the trail, and set on fire. From a limb directly over it dangled a body, head down, its feet fastened to the charred limb by trace chains.

Juan Bujac touched his hat to the grisly spectacle. "Your pardon, poor fool!" he murmured. He had his guns out, and he stared carefully all around. "Indians, or—?"

Mike swallowed the bitter gorge that rose in his throat. The Dutchman had been a harmless kind of man, by and large. Didn't own a weapon, not even a shotgun. And they had roasted him, like a pig on a spit, for the crime of belonging with a Texas trail outfit that showed fight. "Jay-hawkers!"

"Indians or Jayhawkers, I hope they shot him first."

"Then they wouldn't have gone to this trouble."

"True—unless they meant it to warn us. To scare us. To shake our nerves. I admit it turns my stomach!"

"Me *también,*" Mike said mechanically. "Ride back and swing the herd off the trail, wide round out of sight and smell of this. We'd never get 'em past here. I'd sooner the crew didn't see it, either."

"Won't they have to be told? No chuck wagon. No supplies. No cook."

"Yeah, but first I'll get Bruno down and bury him. Catch up with you later."

"Eyes sharp! These *animaluchos* can't be far off. They could be very close. If they come at you—"

"That," Mike said, "is asking for luck!"

Juan moved to his horse. "You would need it!"

In the morning, after making camp, Mike called the crew together and gave out the bad news, skipping the details of Bruno's death. The men already had guessed that the chuck wagon was gone forever, a couple of the flanking riders having glimpsed the reflected glare of it in the night, and their guesses more or less filled in what Mike left out. It was a somber crew, two or three of the younger ones looking sick.

"Butcher a steer and roast it in strips," he told them, wincing slightly over the word "roast," hoping it went unnoticed. "We're going back to day-driving. We'll lay up here for a couple hours' rest, and push on."

"Hard on the cows," Juan said to him privately. "It will take work to head them up out of here. They'll give us trouble."

"Hard on everybody," Mike agreed. "But we've to keep changing over."

"Confuse the enemy by doing the unexpected, eh? Avoid the predictable pattern. Very good tactics in war, love, and poker, my friend—as long as your next move is a secret."

"You hit it on the head, but that's our only bet. I'm trying not to give 'em the time and place to set up an ambush."

"If only we could move faster!" Juan sighed. "They know where we are. I feel we're watched. Can anything we do here confuse them?"

"Not here, no," Mike admitted. "We can quit the regular trail today, though, and strike out on our own. Won't give 'em much chance from ambush if they don't know our route."

Their anticipations of trouble with the herd proved correct. Having settled down after traveling all night, the cattle didn't want to budge again so soon. Irritated, upset in their habits, steers planted their feet and bellowed, others sulked, and some had to be cut back in from trying to scatter. It was nearing noon before the sweating riders got the herd strung out and underway.

Further trouble arose from quitting the regular trail. Brushy creeks and woods caused the cattle column to bunch or break up, and encouraged sidewise wandering. Riders swore in exasperation, horses caught the edgy mood, and like a disease it spread to the cattle. The men on point became unsure of their direction whenever they lost sight of Mike scouting ahead, so Mike had to keep dropping back to guide them. The swing riders botched their teamwork when the herd bent for a change in course and all but made two herds of it. Flankers blamed one another for failing to block wanderers.

Loping out forward to Mike, Juan snapped, dark annoyance on his face, "Your Texans need you! Their nerves are strained by what happened to the cook—by what may be ahead, by lack of sleep, everything."

"Can't you straighten 'em out?"

"I tried. They let me know that I am a Mexican, for the first time this trip."

Mike grunted, nodded. "Take my place, will you? We're about a mile the side of the big trail. Keep it that way."

He rode back to the herd, frowning over the men's affront to Juan, yet not surprised by it. The old feeling existed, at times dormant, then bursting blindly forth under the pressure of nerves, stress, bad temper. The wonder was that Juan, a pistolero, had kept his temper from flashing. Things would never be the same again between him and the crew. The easy give-and-take was ended, just as it was when Mexicans in ill-humor let a Texan know that he was a gringo.

Mike jogged down one side of the herd and up the other, talking quietly to the riders as if nothing was wrong, pulling the outfit together. He had known other outfits to go to pieces, with less cause, everybody hating everybody else.

The point riders were shouting back and forth in argument over the direction when Mike got back up to them, and he asked the one on his side, "Which way did Bujac go?"

"We'd like to know!" the man shot back. "He took off soon after you left him."

Mike kept his face blank. He had taken his time going up and down the strung-out mile of cattle, riding and visiting leisurely to give the men the impression that he hadn't a serious worry on his mind. It was over an hour since he left Juan to scout out the best course and guide the leaders. "No sign of him since?"

The point rider shook his head. "That Mexican's lit out, you ask me! Or maybe he's in with the Jayhawkers!"

Mike looked at him. "Let's don't act like sorry boys a long way from home!" he said. "The man will be back."

But Juan Bujac did not come back.

As the afternoon waned and his segundo did not reappear, Mike gave up trying to fend off his misgivings. He didn't doubt Juan's loyalty. Nor did he believe, as some of the crew professed to believe, that the cook's fate had rattled him into deserting the outfit. That he had met up with trouble was more likely, but that sharp pistolero wasn't apt to get downed without a hard fight, and no shots had been heard. The best that Mike could hope for him was that he had quit, disliking today's flare-up of prejudice.

He dropped back to the point riders. "Aim for that high hill up yonder," he told them. "I'll be locating tonight's bedding ground."

The country stayed brushy and wooded, but the high hill and lower hills by it looked open. He shook up his horse to a lope toward them, and had scarcely left the herd behind him when he came upon Juan Bujac.

At first he didn't recognize anything about the half-naked, bloody object. It hung strung up by its bound wrists, the rope looped over an oak limb, so that it seemed to stand with bended knees and bowed head as if in supplication. Stripped to the waist, the body was a mass of raw flesh.

Mike reined over to it, his stomach a cold knot. He raised the drooping head up by its black hair, stared for a long minute into the dead face, and slowly lowered it again. And still he sat in his saddle, deaf to the oncoming herd, staring down at the battered remains of Juan Bujac, unable to believe that the pistolero had actually fallen victim to the vengeance of the Jayhawkers.

By some trick they had caught him off his guard. Roped him. Taken his guns, his horse and saddle, even his boots and hat. Stripped off his shirt and strung him up. Flogged and beaten him to death.

A piece of paper was tucked into his belt. Mike reached down mechanically and plucked it out. It was apparently a page torn from somebody's tally book. He looked at three words scrawled on it, reading them over and over until the import of them, the hideous mockery of justice, penetrated his sense:

Tried—Sentenced—Executed.

CHAPTER FOUR

The leading steers sniffed the air and rolled their eyes, nervously scenting blood. Riders dropped out to gather and stare with Mike at the body. One, youthful, gulped and threw up.

Mig Apodaca took off his hat, saying with sorrowful respect, "He was hidalgo."

Mike wet his lips. "He was once a somebody, eh?"

"Hidalgo," Mig Apodaca repeated. His burning eyes searched the ground at the body's bare feet. "This was not done here."

"How d'you know?"

"Such a beating must splash blood all round. There is none."

"You're right," Mike said. "They brought him here afterwards and hung him up for us to see." His rage gave way to swift thought. "Wasn't long ago—only minutes! They watched and made sure we'd come by here! They're up to something!"

The leading steers had stalled and those following were bunching up, snorting and bawling, all heads turned toward the east as if unseen devils rode the wind. "What do they smell now?" asked a rider, and sniffed. "What do *I* smell?"

Mike caught it in his nostrils, acrid and tingling, a smell that reminded him of an Indian stampeding trick of burning a sack of buffalo hair on the windward side of a herd. The smoke of it, no matter how thin, permeated the air over a wide area and drove cattle frantic with fear of the unknown.

"Back to the herd! Swing 'em west any way you can— jump to it!" He blamed himself for letting the men group up while half the herd went untended. Finding the body of Juan Bujac like that had jarred him out of his ordinary vigilance. It came to him that the Jayhawkers had counted on just such a lapse.

He sensed a stampede in the making, building up fast. The cattle were ready for it. The sun was low, and in the long shadows of the trees their eyes burned like bull's-eye lanterns. He could feel the crazy-mad spirit of them, straining for something to set them off—a man's falling hat, the stumble of a horse, anything.

He and the men with him were trying to work the forward end of the herd into some kind of shape, when down at the other end a chorus of wolflike howls shattered the last shreds of cow sense. The leaders jumped and lit out. The bulk of the herd came roaring in mad waves, scattering men and horses. A rider fired his gun in a forlorn attempt to turn the stampede. There was only the muzzle flash, no sound of the report. A shot couldn't be heard in the thunder of earth-shaking hoofs, blaring steers, and clashing horns.

Mike's horse changed ends under him and was off in a dead run. A wise *grulla,* it sought to stay ahead of the avalanche of charging cattle and lean off to one side, but dodging around a brush clump it ran into a pocket, steers hard on its trail.

The brush looked too thick for a bird to build its nest in. Mike went down on the grulla's neck and they crashed into it. Shielding his face and eyes from the thorns, he felt the grulla dodging and scrambling, and twice he was almost dragged off before they broke through.

"Godamighty!" he muttered dismally, clinging to the thought of trying to get the herd to circling, while his senses insisted that the herd must have split up. Even the grulla acted undecided on which direction to take. The worst had happened, and in the chaos one place wasn't much better than another.

Three horsemen made up his mind for him, bursting from an oak grove seventy yards distant and recognizing him on sight. They hauled up and slid rifles from saddle scabbards, in preference to six-guns at shorter range. Not lingering to unshuck his own rifle and duel it out with them, he took off from there to find what he could of the herd.

A bullet screamed over his head. The rifle shot came from his left. Against the glow of the sinking sun he spied two more horsemen at halt, then again he was crashing through brush, the grulla choosing the course and seeming to know where it was going.

The noise of cattle dulled, drawing off to a heavy rumble pierced by thin yells. Mike cursed the wolf-howling stampeders. They still were hard at it, giving the steers no chance to shed their wild terror, chasing them miles off everywhere.

"Godamighty!" he muttered again. "Where's my crew?"

Another sound rose, of faster cadence—that of a running band of horses. The grulla raced on toward the sound, jumping gulches and splitting brush, and came up alongside the remuda. As an achievement of the senses, or of unerring instinct, it was a fine feat, and Mike guessed his horse was proud of itself, but in the fading light he picked out a dozen or more mounted men riding behind.

The grulla wished to travel along with its trail mates. Mike disagreed. A man shouted a sharp warning. The riders promptly came swinging around the remuda. Mike got off a shot, and wheeled his unwilling horse. He drew half a dozen shots for his one, which hastened the grulla to lay back its ears and flatten out, forsaking the captured remuda.

Mid-morning next day Mike tracked four men of his crew to a gulch where they were hiding with their horses. One man had a bullet hole through his shoulder. His name was Tom Spettel, and this was his first trip up the trail. It would be his last, he vowed, if this one ran to pattern.

"I stayed with a bunch o' cows till some bastard shot me! And after Branch picked me up they hunted us half the night." Branch Sherrill was his sidekick, an older man who spoke little. "God, what a bust!"

"I didn't get to sleep much myself," Mike said. "Anybody know about the rest?"

Bob Hindes, picking thorns out of his legs, looked up and nodded. He was young, usually cheerful, though not now. "I talked with some of 'em early this morning. Them and the others are going on up to Abilene. I woulda gone along, only I was looking for Gus, here. We'll start up tonight."

"To Abilene? With no cows?"

"Might be a feller can catch a job there."

Branch Sherrill spoke up, for once. "Puttin' it plain, we're ashamed to go back home. All of us. We lost the herd."

"I'm the one responsible," Mike reminded him. "I'm trail boss of the outfit."

Tom Spettel took it up. "Boss o' nothing, Mike! She's gone

to hell—herd, remuda, chuck wagon! I ain't the only one took damage. Bob says half the rest's got hurts, one kind or 'nother. We only got a horse apiece, and they're pretty tore up. No, I sure wouldn't want to face the home-folks."

"Nor me!" Bob Hinds said. "They're busted flat now. Poor Byler put a bad crimp in the Lost Creek folks—but we've laid 'em out where they'll never get well! And us prancin' so gay how we'd pull 'em out o' the hole! I ain't *never* goin' back home!"

"How 'bout you?" Branch Sherrill asked Mike.

Mike shook his head. "Got to see about the herd."

"I'll tell you right where it is," Tom Spettel said. "It's scattered all over the Indian Territory!"

"Guess so, but I'm not going off and leaving it."

"Man, you're crazy! It's touched you in the head! What did they do to the cook? What did they do to the Mexican? What would they think up for *you,* they catch you?"

Mike had loosened cinch and aired the saddle. Now he tightened it, not replying. About to mount, he paused. He dug out his money belt. It contained his personal emergency fund, cash to be used in last resort. It wasn't much, and he didn't look forward to buying anything in the brush. He tossed the money belt to Branch Sherrill.

"Share it among the others when you meet up with 'em."

"You mean you're goin' back there? Now?"

He legged aboard the tired grulla. "Well," he said in sparse explanation, reining it around, "I've got to be doing something. . . ."

At the end of his third day of prowling, Mike Gould made camp in the lee of a flat rock formation that afforded some shelter from a rising night-wind. He built a fire, skinned and dressed out the cottontail rabbit he had shot that day, and proceeded without much zest to roast it on the pointed end of a stick. His taste tired of rabbit as a steady diet. While it gave nourishment, it soon grew monotonous. His horse fared little better, having no grain, but there was plenty of grass and he took care not to work it too hard.

Throughout the area he had found no cattle, horses, or men. Only tracks. Tomorrow, he decided, he would fasten onto a set of those tracks and follow them through. It might well be that they would all come together somewhere. The Jayhawkers hadn't stampeded the herd for the sheer hell of it; they had ridden on after the spooked cattle, perhaps to

32 L. L. Foreman

round up and drive to some selected holding spot where brands could be burned over. They weren't interested in fever ticks.

The wind gusted past the flat rock and stirred up eddies in its shelter. Fanning smoke from his face, he turned the spitted rabbit over the fire; it was starting to brown.

And if, he thought, I find the herd, what can I do about it? Go for the law? Federal men carry the only smidge of law there is here. United States marshals. I haven't seen sign of one yet.

A flurry of hoofbeats snapped him out of his barren musings. Thinking that he had the area to himself, he had thrown off the saddle and hobbled the grulla out to graze, lighted his fire with slight concern, and not strained his ears to listen beyond the booming of the wind. He snatched his rifle. From his squatting position he dived out of the firelight and scrambled around the flat rock.

Pounding up into the wind, the riders pulled to a halt and sat motionless, four men dimly seen at the outer edge of the firelight. By their stillness they conveyed the impression of alert vigilance, a readiness to cut loose at the first hint of hostility. At last one of them sent forward a mocking hail.

"Hello-oo, the camp!"

"Light down and come in!" Mike called.

"Ready for company?"

"You know it! Let me see you!"

They nudged their horses forward a few steps. "We ain't marshals, if that's your worry," drawled the speaker. He wore a soiled bandage aslant his forehead and half over one eye, his hat dangled behind by its chin strings. All four bore the stamp of sharp-edged men, their faces saturnine, eyes insolent and at the same time wary, and Mike placed them as gunmen. Down-at-heel gunmen, he amended, taking in the shabby state of their garb.

He stepped out from cover, making his every movement slow and deliberate, his rifle upended across his chest. The eyes of the watching foursome reflected a knowing appreciation of his carefulness. He glanced at the fire. In it, the blackened carcass of the rabbit sizzled and sputtered.

"Dammit, you made me ruin my supper!" he growled. "Look at that!"

They looked, dismounting. "Poverty camp," one commented in disgust. "An' we hoped you might be a cussed Texan takin' home cow-money!"

He stopped by Mike's saddle on the ground, eyeing its double cinch and short maguey rope tied fast to the saddle-horn.

"A Texas rig!" he said meaningfully, and all four stood stockstill, instantly braced for action.

CHAPTER FIVE

Mike said, "Yeah. Was riding for a Panhandle outfit, till a nosy marshal showed up. I lit out on the ramrod's horse."

"Makes a good story, short an' sweet!"

"You calling me a liar?" There was only one way to handle this challenge, and that was to fling the challenge back, risking a fight. A hungry man on the dodge was all too likely to unleash a touchy temper.

The bandaged man came a step closer. He cocked his head to see Mike better with his half-covered eye, studying him. "I don't recommend you get snorty!"

"You ruined my supper, busting up on me that fool way! Damn right I'm snorty!"

"There's four of us. We're a leetle on the scrap, too!"

"You serving me warning?"

"That's close."

"Go to hell!"

The bandaged man unexpectedly burst out a laugh. "Boys, he's all right! I ain't seen him in years, but I don't forget a face like his! An' the way he says 'go to hell' sets him square in my rec'lection. Howdy, Gould! Don't know me— Ritchie McChristal? We rid guard for that crazy goldmine outfit in Arizona. It was way off where the panther laid down an' died. The Apaches picked off our horses, ev'ry last one, an' we—"

"Let *him* tell it, Mac," one of the others cut in. "You could be mistook."

Mike nodded. "I remember. Stranded us all afoot, west of the Superstition Mountains. Outfit broke up and we never

34

did draw our pay." He shook hands. "Didn't know you under that rag. What happened to your head?"

"Skinned it on a low branch in the dark. Boys, break out the beef an' biscuits! Get the jug!"

They built up the fire and loafed around it, eating and passing the jug of whiskey. Ritchie McChristal, as Mike remembered him, had been a straightforward gunhand who hired out to anybody as long as the job didn't put him too wide of the law. Not any more. In the few years since, he had become an outlaw and a badman. Taking it for granted that Mike had gone the same route, he discussed recent activities.

"We went to robbin' trains in Missouri," he told Mike, "but it got hot an' we had to ki-yi down here. Was nine of us. The marshals took the others. Tough? Man, that was a hungry ride across Missouri an' down Kansas, the posses on our tails. My gut got that shrunk it wouldn't chamber a liver pill. Lost our takin's."

Mike drank from the jug. "You eating regular now?"

"Aim to. We're throwin' in with these Jayhawkers. They rule the roost here, an' they got a helluva good game, raidin' the Texas trail herds. Four days back they took nigh on two thousand head at one crack. Hell, that's 'bout seventy-five thousand dollars in the northern markets! We lent a hand, to show 'em our heart's in the right place."

"You get a share?" Mike asked casually.

"Just grub an' firewater, an' a dab o' cash. It'll come better when we're fixed in. We got there too late to make the stompede, but we heard it. Helped round 'em up later. That's how I skinned my head. Like to've knocked my brains out." McChristal touched his injured head gently.

"Maybe you did," said one of his three companions. They squatted together on the far side of the fire, unsmiling.

"Talk about your stompedes!" McChristal went on. "They ran half the night. We stayed with 'em, us an' the Jayhawkers. When those cows hit the rocks you could hear their feet clackin' like sharpenin' up a million butcher knives. You shoulda been there!"

"Next time, maybe."

"Sure, why not? Pass the jug." He gulped down the raw whiskey and blew a long breath. "We ain't fixed right in with 'em yet, but it won't be long. They sent us back here to comb for strays. Hell, they didn't leave no strays, not them! Didn't want us to know where they driv the herd to."

"Don't trust you?" Mike asked.

"That ain't it," McChristal denied. "We stand in okay with one bunch, but another bunch came in on the job an' they didn't know us. They natchally wasn't sure 'bout us. Said we hadn't got the nod from the 'big feller' yet, far's they knew."

He shut tight his eyes and opened them wide again, muttering, "Startin' to see two o' you, an' that's one too much. Know when I've had enough." He corked the jug firmly. "They run in bands, y'know, like them Apache war parties did in Arizona. Job gets too tough for one, they send out the call for others."

"I know." On a blind guess, Mike added, "The 'big feller,' he's like the big chief. The kingpin."

"He's sure got 'em lined up, I'll tell you that! Use' ta be, they say, they rattled round loose. Now they ride under his orders. It pays 'em to. Look at the setup he's got! His big spread's spang-handy on the Kansas line, and he keeps a headquarters below it somewhere east o' here. Figger that out!"

Mike yawned as if hearing stale news. He was aware that the three men across the fire, silent, were measuring him. Train robbers, carrying bounty on their heads, distrusted strangers. Mike noted that they drank sparingly when the jug passed their way.

"It's a big operation," he commented. Stolen cattle could be held at the headuqarters, awaiting the opportune time to be shifted safely up onto the Kansas ranch. That took no figuring.

McChristal forgetfully uncorked the jug and drank. He wiped his mouth. "Ain't nothin' small 'bout Earl Hollinger!"

The name meant nothing to Mike. He stored it in his mind, remarking, "Big man, all right, that Earl Hollinger. Got lots o' savvy."

McChristal frowned at him. "You put on like you know it all! Like I can't tell you nothin' 'bout Hollinger you don't know better!" He squinted challengingly. "All right—you tell me how he sells off all them Texas cows!"

"Most any brand can be worked over, and it's no trick to alter an earmark. All you need is a holding spot, good brand artists, and plenty time." As he said it, Mike sensed that he had given a wrong answer. The three silent men regarded him cynically.

"Called your bluff!" McChristal reached over unsteadily and poked him in the ribs. "Gould, you stepped into that like a bull moose in a beartrap! Oh, sure, there's brand changing now an' then," he granted, "but you ain't no-where's near right."

Mike brought up a grin. "Can't score every time."

"Not off me, you can't!" McChristal grinned back, his good humor restored. "This man Hollinger's got tricks you never heard of. He holds contracts to deliver shipments o' dressed beef to Injun reservations. Gov'ment contracts. They call for maybe five thousand head the year round. Dressed beef, mind, paid by weight."

"Skinned and dressed. All right." Mike nodded. "But what about the hides? He's required by law to show the hides with every beef delivery, I know that much. They have to pass inspection at the Indian Agency. They're counted, and a close check's made on the brands. Then they go to the hide yard."

"Right! So how does Hollinger get round that? Here's the trick. He makes a beef shipment of his own cows, the gen-uwine article. The hides pass inspection an' the beef's de-livered, all straight an' aboveboard. Then after dark, Hollin-ger's men go an' load those hides back in the wagon an' carry 'em off. Same hides are showed to get shipments o' stolen beef past the inspectors. They pull the trick over an over, usin' those same hides long's they can keep 'em lookin' fresh."

"Wait a minute," Mike said. "Somebody'd soon holler that the hide yard was short of hides."

McChristal slapped the jug fondly, laughing. "You ain't smart! The hides off the stolen cows are smuggled in to make up the shortage. Nobody ever inspects 'em again before they're baled up an' shipped out to the tanners. The feller who runs the hide yard, he gets the hides for nothin' an' keeps his mouth shut."

Mike thought of his herd. By such trickery nineteen hun-dred head of steers could soon be made to vanish without a trace, passed under the hoodwinked eyes of the Indian Agency inspectors, and sold on government contracts at the market price for butchered beef. The thought galled him into saying unguardedly, "It's one hell of a year for Texans!"

The saturnine threesome exchanged brief glances, rising to their feet. McChristal, though, too drunk to catch the drift, said, "Couldn't be better for Jayhawkers! Whatcha think o' that trick, Gould? Ain't she slick? Some o' the bunch told us 'bout it. We was layin' round drinkin', an' they got to runnin' off at the mouth."

"Like what you're doing now!" snapped one of the three.

McChristal turned on him. "Goddam it, I'm talkin' with an old sidekick! We rid together years ago!"

"What's he done since?"

"It ain't polite to ask! Sit down!" He turned back to Mike. "Don't pay 'em no mind. They're that spooky they shy at their own shadders." He drank, handed Mike the jug, and with grunting effort he got up and lurched off to relieve himself behind the flat rock.

"Injun beef," he muttered, coming back. "Funny thing. There's one Injun tribe Hollinger won't let no beef go to. The Round Mountain Pawnees. No beef for them, not at any damn price."

"What's his reason?" Mike asked him.

McChristal shook his head. "Dunno. Jayhawkers already busted two herds bound for Round Mountain this year. They say another herd's comin' up. It won't never get there. Hollinger's orders. He won't contract beef for them Pawnees, an' he ain't about to let nobody else do it."

He stretched out on the ground. The night was far advanced. Before falling asleep, he mumbled, "We got a camp, couple hours' ride from here. Nester's shack. You string 'long with us, huh?"

Not able at the moment to invent any reason for refusing, Mike answered, "Well—if it's all right with your friends, here."

The three eyed him fixedly. The one who had spoken before said softly, "It's just fine. Suits us just fine."

Once more Mike made out on short and light sleep, sitting up with his back to the rock. The wind died. His least movement drew the instant attention of three pairs of eyes. He was relieved when McChristal woke up toward morning and, either forgetting his offer or regretting it, announced that he and his three companions had better get started back to their camp.

The three balked. They reminded McChristal that he had invited Mike to share their camp. Solemnly, they raised the point of common hospitality. You didn't leave an old sidekick to coyote out in the brush, if you had a roof to offer him.

Seeing that they were set on making an issue of it, Mc-

Christal said heartily, "Sure, Gould, come on with us!"

But his tone rang false. A restraint had come over his manner. Mike guessed that he was harking back to his loose talk while drinking. Sober, he was taking account of the knowledge that he had revealed. Dangerous knowledge. His restraint meant that he had caught the mood of his three fellow outlaws, was perhaps even examining a suspicion that Mike had worked the auger and pried the information out of him. The paths of gunslingers often branched wide apart over the years. A friend of the past could become an enemy of the present—an undercover law officer, a ruthless bounty hunter, a spy or cattlemen's detective.

They obligingly caught Mike's hobbled horse for him. They watched him saddle and bridle it and slide his rifle into the boot, and noted how he hitched his holster forward when mounting. By unspoken agreement he drew the position alongside McChristal, the other three riding behind abreast.

Keeping me under close watch, he thought, till they find out more about me. Mac would like to forget the whole thing, give me the benefit of the doubt for old time's sake. Not them. They'd gun me in the back right now, if it wasn't for Mac. On the other hand, Mac will side with them if there's a showdown.

Breaking a strained and lengthy silence, McChristal said to Mike, "Our shack ain't big, but we got room for you any ol' time." Furthering his attempt to make friendly conversation, he added, "Jayhawkers took the nester out an' hanged him, early spring."

"Why?"

"Suspicioned he was a Texan."

"Was he?"

"Damn if I know. Anyhow, he threw up a tight lil' shack."

Mike nodded. "Bet I'll be right comfortable."

The tight little shack stood in a clearing on the bank of a small stream. As a homestead it was a pretty spot, a secluded spot, distant from any beaten trail. The hapless nester who put in his labor hadn't lived to finish it, for the tree stumps remained in the ground.

A saddled black horse faced the open door of the shack, its reins tied to a foreleg, Northern style. Threading through the surrounding trees and thick undrgrowth into the clearing, McChristal looked ahead at the black horse and spoke to the three men riding behind.

"Witter's here waitin' for us. What d'you bet we're fin'ly gettin' the nod? Boys, we're fixed up! We're full-blowed Jay-hawkers!"

"Him, too? Gould?"

"Not right off, no, you know that. He'll have to sweat a spell, same's we done. You aim to talk him down?"

"Witter's got the say-so, not us."

A man stepped to the door of the shack as they started across the stump-studded clearing. He was hairy-faced, heavily armed with two belted guns and a knife, and carried a .44 Henry repeating rifle, too long to fit into any saddle boot ever made. But the first thing about him that brought Mike's attention leaping was that he wore Juan Bujac's hat.

"Hi, there, Witter!" McChristal sang out.

Witter lowered his head, peering at them from under the wide brim of the hat. They had swung in from the east; the early sun shone behind them and he was trying to shade the glare of it from his eyes. "Who's that you got with you?" he demanded.

Passing a stump, Mike thumbed the grulla to make it shy as if something about the stump startled it. His intention was to maneuver himself away from McChristal, drop out from in front of the three, and get set to make a break for it. Although he was acquainted with the grulla's touchy disposition, he banked on it not to raise a fit at the thumbing.

The next instant he was clamping the deck of a pitching bronc. The outraged grulla threw a high-roller, sunfished in mid-air, and came down swapping ends. Not having expressed its annoyance sufficiently, it reared up pawing, then went to bucking in circles. The other horses promptly fell into the spirit and broke up the formation.

Hauling on the reins of his plunging horse, McChristal called, "What the hell's got into your broomtail, Gould?"

Whirling dizzily, Mike caught a flash of Witter raising the long .44 Henry. He heard him shout, "Goddam if it ain't that Texas trail boss!"

He jerked out his gun and fired, but already he was spinning in another direction on the back of the pitching grulla. The heavy rifle boomed. Witter was finding much the same trouble, trying to hit an elusive target. The black shied away from the close discharge and hopped on three legs, tugging at its tied reins. Witter stepped after it, but kept the rifle to his shoulder, waiting for the grulla to quit bouncing in circles.

The next time around, Mike slung two fast shots, one on the bear-down, one on the go-away. He saw Witter drop the rifle and trip forward over it, the Mexican hat sliding off his head.

Two guns cracked, two of the three men trying to make score from pitching horse to pitching horse, the third man jumping off his heaving saddle to halve the predicament and taking a running sprawl. McChristal hadn't drawn a gun, although his horse was giving less trouble than the rest. He did now, screaming, "Damn you, Gould, you've killed Witter!"

The grulla suddenly planted itself stiff-legged, shivering as if taking blame for the whole eruption of horse-mischief and gunfire. Mike squalled an Apache yell and spurred it full at McChristal, who instinctively wrenched his horse aside. Reining off in a tight turn and lining out for the woods, Mike looked back to see McChristal and the dismounted man taking aim after him.

He fired twice. Later, weaving through the trees and brush at a headlong run, he guessed something had caused him to miss McChristal on purpose, sending his bullet only close enough to make him duck and spoil his aim. Old sidekick. A badman now, but he wasn't then. He was going to have trouble explaining the matter of bringing a marked Texan into camp and the killing of Witter. Maybe he'd take the simpler course of dodging clear out of the Indian Territory.

Either way, Ritchie McChristal wasn't ever likely to make the Jayhawker grade. He had talked too free and pulled a bobble. Well and good. Any small gain gratefully received. Somewhere eastward, he'd said, Earl Hollinger, that mighty kingpin of the Jayhawkers, had a headquarters and holding spot for plundered Texas herds. Mike bore easterly.

And blessed be the bullet that felled Witter, wearing Juan Bujac's hat. "I got one of 'em for you, *compadre*," he said aloud. It didn't ease the sad anger, nor dull the memory of how Juan died.

CHAPTER SIX

From the high crest of a thinly wooded hill, Mike Gould surveyed a trail herd winding up from the south—the only herd he had seen in a week's search—and knowing it to be the Cullen herd from Lost Creek, he could imagine the setbacks that had delayed it so far behind schedule. The wonder was that it had got this far.

He stared down with the cold eyes of a man on the make, seeing the outfit as a Jonah stumbling to ruin, wasting no sympathy on Harley Cullen for hiring hardcases instead of experienced trail drivers. Up front, the pair of men on point rode too close and out of line, causing the lead steers to swerve nervously from side to side. The swing riders hung too far back, allowing the column of cattle to bend and bunch up, and the men on flank dawdled practically within speaking distance of those who were supposed to be bringing up the drag. The remuda straggled way behind.

Two wagons trundled ahead, one the chuck wagon, the other a canvas-topped affair almost the size of a prairie schooner. The mismanaged herd had evidently kicked up plenty of trouble. These steers hadn't fallen into steady habits, hadn't had the chance. Bad handling had about ruined them for the trail. They constantly mingled, restless and wayward, bawling, shaking their horns. It was clear that they had recently stampeded, remembered it, and were hysterically ready to pop off again for any reason or none at all.

Furthermore, the outfit had somehow lost itself, apparently. It had strayed far off any route known to Mike, and was blundering through untracked country, angling toward the river where the high banks would prohibit crossing.

"Greeners," Mike muttered, and shrugged, absently patting the neck of his grulla horse. The grulla quivered, shooting its ears knowingly at the color-splotched ribbon of cattle stretched out below. "The damn-fool greeners!"

Permitting himself no forgiveness for his own failures, he spared small tolerance on the errors of others. Life had toughened him early. The disaster that had lately struck at him had smashed his bid for fortune, ruined his Lost Creek neighbors, and left him worse than broke, but he could not accept defeat. By some means or other he had to recoup at least a part of his losses, to take back to Eb Saunders and Parson and the rest.

So he stared down at the derelict Cullen outfit with a predatory glint awakening in his eyes. Most likely, straying adrift into this rough country was all that had saved it from falling afoul of the Jayhawker gangs. The dumb luck of ignorance. Luck that couldn't last. The same ignorance would wreck the outfit. It was inevitable.

If he could contrive to gain some profit from the wreck, salvage something from it for himself . . . He nodded slowly to the thought. Why not? The outfit was doomed, anyway. And Cullen, that well-heeled Yankee, had fouled him up, buying cattle and supplies that were promised to him.

Two men rode ahead of the wagons. They evidently were scouting the route, but weren't anywhere near far enough forward to judge the next mile. One of them, short and heavily built, bearded, Mike easily recognized as Harley Cullen; he still wore his flat-brimmed hat and black coat, and sat his horse solidly. The other was tall and thin, coatless, big-hatted, and rode with lounging ease.

Mike nudged the grulla and cut aslant down the hill toward them. In their upflung faces he saw surprise, followed immediately by wariness. Here in the Indian Territory, deep in the roughs at that, a lone rider was a rarity, therefore suspect, and he was aware that his ragged and hard-used appearance stood against him. To their eyes he guessed he could have been a badman on the dodge, a spy for cattle raiders, a Jayhawker, anything.

He reined around facing them, and they pulled up. They watched him pat the neck of the grulla, and their regard searched at his holstered gun, then played over him. His scarecrow garb, spotted and grimed by campfire and the dirt of many days in and out of the brush, did not conceal his muscular compactness. Above a heavy bristle his dark gray eyes returned their regard. He saw that Cullen hadn't yet recognized him, and shoved back the ruin of his hat.

"Mr. Gould!" Cullen said in his sober fashion, without warmth.

"Mr. Cullen," Mike responded, equally cool. "Who's your trail boss, if you've got one?"

The curtness of the question ruffled Cullen into drawing his brows together. He motioned at his tall companion. "Phin Starr, here. Why?"

Mike met Phin Starr's stare, measuring its sharp hostility. A sour-looking man, the trail boss, thin-lipped. Quick on the scrap, no doubt, like the rest of Cullen's Kansans or whatever they were. "You ever make the trail before?"

"Not this one," Starr allowed. He studied again the hang of Mike's gun, speculatively. "That any o' your business?"

"Not a damn bit," Mike said. "It's no concern to me that you've run this herd into a godforsaken bobble. Neither does it break me up that you had a stampede couple nights back, and lost a bunch."

Harley Cullen exclaimed wonderingly, "How did you know that?" Without waiting for a reply, he said, "Trouble, trouble, all the way! One thing after another. That last stampede was the worst. Yes, we're around two hundred short." He shook his head. "This drive worries me, everything going wrong. We're behind time, and now it seems to me we took the wrong direction. I'm new to this," he explained.

"That," Mike said, "I could easy believe, if I didn't already know it. But I'm curious why you didn't hunt up your missing cows."

"Starr's positive they ran north to the river. We expect to pick them up along there."

"The lazy man's way, eh?" Mike commented.

He could understand it of Cullen, who didn't even sit his saddle like a man of the range. To a greener, the hit-or-miss procedure could sound reasonable. Phin Starr, though, bore the stamp of a cowman, and it rang a wrong note that he should give way to such slovenly handling of cattle in his charge. It raised the thought that perhaps Starr had marked off the herd as lost in any case, and felt that a couple of hundred head more or less didn't much matter.

Starr said, "No, the smart man's way. I'm hired to boss this drive, an' I know what I'm doing."

"I wouldn't hire you to tend goats in a backyard," Mike told him bluntly. To Cullen, he said, "The route you're headed, you'll never come on your missing cows. They didn't stay by the river—the high banks turned 'em. They drifted till—"

"Mister," Starr drawled in mock admiration, "you sure do 'pear to know all about it! Us, now, we couldn't even tell what set off that stampede. Would you know that, too, maybe?"

Mike's eyes glimmered in the sudden dark flare of his face. "Speak your meaning out plain," he said softly, "and I'll take you on!"

Harley Cullen raised a protesting hand. "Gould, you beat up one of my men already!"

"He needed it, like this one!"

Starr's thin lips spread straight and tight. "I got a mind to call you on that!"

"I'm waiting."

"I ain't no Texas gunslinger."

Mike unbuckled his gun belt and hung it on the saddle-horn. "Got fists, haven't you?"

"I sure have!" Starr jumped from his horse. Not pausing to shuck his gun belt, he rushed at Mike while he was still dismounting. "An' here they are, stampeder!"

His thickened, blue-scarred knuckles gave evidence of many a barefisted brawl. His first blow slammed Mike into the grulla, and the startled horse reared and knocked him away. Starr closed in and brought up a knee.

Thrown off balance, the only way for Mike to avoid a crippling knee-dig in the groin was to fall back and go down. He landed in gravel, and saw Starr coming instantly after him. Starr took a long stride, bending his right leg for a full, swinging kick. The man was out to maim him at once, then finish him off.

Mike rolled fast over. He fended the kick with his lean rump, slewed himself around on the ground, and lunged upward with both spread feet. One high heel cracked Starr below the knee, the other boot met him in mid-body as he tripped forward. Starr abruptly fell aside on his hands and knees, teeth bared in pain, thin lips wincing. Mike sprang up and, barely giving him time to rise, hit him a backhand wallop across the bridge of his nose. He hit him again, a left uppercut under the jaw to straighten him up, and went to work on him.

Both wagons had halted. The leading cattle were coming up, and two men on point, seeing the fight, came spurring

on ahead. Harley Cullen shouted at Mike, "Quit it, Gould
—quit it! He's had enough!"

Starr had had enough and more, but he wasn't disposed to
let it end at that. He tottered back, legs sagging, made as if
to turn away in defeat, and dug at his holstered gun.

Mike stepped in and put everything he had into one last,
straight-arm piledriver. Gasping, bloody-faced, Starr dropped
stretched out. He had taken a fearful beating and it was plain
to see he would not be much good for anything useful for a
long time to come.

The two riders jolted to a halt, swung down, and advanced to pitch in for their downed trail boss. Mike picked
up Starr's gun and moved to meet them. His violent mood
unslaked, his temper brittle, he rasped a challenge and a
high-handed command.

"You ducks want a whirl at it? Make your play, or get on
back to the cows right now! It's a hell of a pair o' pointers
who'll go off leaving the herd to drift!"

They paused, taking a close look at him. "Go back, you
men—go back!" said Cullen anxiously. Muttering, they re-
mounted. Cullen called after them, "Better start bedding 'em
down here. We can't push on any farther today, Starr's hurt
too bad." He turned on Mike. "You've disabled my trail
boss! Look—his eyes are swollen shut! He couldn't see to do
his job, even if he was able to ride!"

Mike eyed him bleakly. "It's not a particle to what he
aimed to do to me, is it? Anyhow, he showed he wasn't able
to pilot and boss this outfit to begin with."

Deliberately, he fed his wrath. "You lost a bunch of cows.
Two hundred and fourteen, by my count. Yes, I found 'em.
I rounded 'em up and choused 'em into a draw, and penned
'em there with brush. That was work. I knew they were
yours, and I took the time to backtrack 'em and search for
your outfit."

"I'm obliged to you," Cullen began, "for your—"

Mike cut him off. "What I get for my trouble is hard talk
and a dirty fight! Did you jerk the bridle on Starr? No, you
gave him free rein." He was overstating the case purposely,
driven by hard necessity to make a claim of which he felt
none too proud. "All right! For a civil word you could've
had your cows. I'm no damn stampeder. But right as of now,
Cullen, you're looking at a Texas mavericker!"

Cullen frowned, uncertain of the significance, while sensing that he was about to be handed the hot end of an iron.

"Just what do you mean by that, Gould?" Had he asked the question good-naturedly, less like a flinty tradesman, he might yet have got his missing cows back for a word of thanks. As it was, his sharp tone steeled Mike.

"I mean," Mike said, "that a mavericker hunts out lost cattle, wild cattle, for a price. In Texas it's around a dollar a head. Sometimes two, depending on the market and how thick's the brasada he's got to work in. Up in this country it ought to run higher, things being as they are, don't you reckon? The market's booming, and where those cows are the country's that rough you'd never find 'em in a month."

"How much?" Cullen snapped.

"Six dollars a head. That's no more'n you paid my hungry neighbors for 'em." Mike figured the total aloud. "Six times two hundred and fourteen makes—h'm, let's see. . . . Twelve hundred and eighty-four dollars, right?"

"Twelve hundred—!" Cullen swallowed. He forced a pinched smile. "You Texans don't lack gall, do you? What you demand is out of all reason! It's nothing short of blackmail!"

Mike walked to his horse and strapped on his gun belt. "If you must haggle, I'll shave it down to an even thousand. That's my bottom offer. You get your cows back, you owe me a thousand dollars. If they're not worth that to you, let 'em go. Either way, I guess you can afford it."

"As a matter of fact, I can't."

And that, Mike guessed, was a barefaced lie. Cullen had paid cash for his herd, for his horses and supplies, and the pay of his picked hardcases certainly ran better than thirty a month. His two wagons had cost money, especially the big one. At his Lost Creek camp he had supported himself in pretty good style. And that girl, his so-called niece, must have been expensive company. He was a Yankee speculator taking a plunge in cattle, attracted by the rising market, grasping an opportunity to buy cheap, expecting to sell dear and pocket a rich profit. An exploiter of small and needy cowmen.

Remembrance of the girl further soured Mike against Cullen. It wasn't right that a man pushing fifty should use his money to buy the company of a young girl. Not a bit right. She hadn't been any dance hall Lulu, nothing like that. A kind of thoroughbred quality about her, he remembered, or thought he did.

"I can't afford it at all," Cullen said. He waited, and observing Mike's disbelief, he added, "You're holding a grudge against me, I see."

Mike shrugged. "I could be. It shouldn't surprise you."

"Because of Starr? My cattle? Those supplies I bought from Peck?"

"Put it this way," Mike said. "My Lost Creek neighbors are working cowmen, like me. They got caught short in the Byler Bust. You came down there and took advantage, buying the rest of their cows dirt cheap, knowing how bad they needed eating-money. You're a speculator, fattening on the misfortunes of others. Nothing you do looks right to me!"

Cullen nodded. "I see. You're wrong about me, or half wrong, but never mind. I'm not interested in trying to change your opinion. Anyway, I think your grudge goes deeper than that."

Starr showed signs of coming to, groaning and mumbling. Cullen looked down at him thoughtfully, giving no more sign of feeling than a man inspecting his played-out horse and cogitating how to replace it with a fresh mount. "Gould," he remarked, "I heard around Lost Creek that you're something of a gambler."

Mike said nothing. Cullen went on, "I've made the statement that a strong fighting crew can get a herd through, regardless of how much trail-driving experience they've had. It may have reached your ears."

"It did."

"Perhaps I miscalculated. Things have been going from bad to worse. These men—"

"They're scalawags!" Mike said shortly, watching their sloppy handling of the herd. Bawling steers milled about the two halted wagons, threatening to scare the teams if the languid riders didn't soon cut them back.

"No," Cullen contradicted him, humorlessly defending his choice of a crew after having admitted its imperfection. "I can't go so far as to say that. They know cattle. They know the Indian Territory. That's why I hired them, as well as for their toughness. It's only that they—well, Starr's been inclined to run a slack outfit."

Slack was right, Mike privately agreed. No order, no organization, every man doing pretty much as he pleased and raising no sweat about it. They were laying off on one another, passing the buck.

Cullen reverted to his former remark. "They said at Lost Creek that you've worked with trail herds. You've been around. You know this country. I know for myself you can fight."

"What's this leading up to?" Mike asked him.

"An offer." He gazed off at the wagons as if for aid in finding the right words. "I want those cows of mine. But I can't pay you a thousand dollars. I haven't got it—won't have it till I finish this drive."

"S'pose you don't finish?"

"I've got to! Too much depends on it!" Cullen brought his eyes to Mike's face. Shrewd eyes, for all their desperate worry. "Is it your opinion we might not make it? Your honest opinion?"

"With this sorry crew," Mike said, "I think you'll lose your herd—and I'll lose a thousand dollars! Yes, that's my honest opinion. You've gone astray in these roughs and don't know what lies ahead. Your herd's got the stampede fever and needs careful handling. Your riders are careless. They may be hot on the scrap, but they don't trail worth a damn. I haven't mentioned Jayhawkers. They can crop up any place, any time."

"You don't soften it, do you?"

"You asked my opinion. I don't hold much hope for that thousand dollars."

"A thousand dollars," Cullen muttered. "It's nothing, to what's at stake. Nothing!" He stared again toward the wagons. "Gould—help me deliver this herd, and I'll make it two thousand!"

Mike surveyed the outfit. "Double or nothing, h'm?" This was more to his taste. A gamble, a long shot. A possible fresh start. "Got paper and pencil, Cullen? Write me a note for two thousand dollars, on the herd. I take the deal on one condition."

"And that is?" Cullen asked, writing on a page of his notebook, signing it, tearing it out.

"That I run the outfit, no argument."

"Agreed. Here's your note."

Tucking the note into his shirt pocket, Mike inquired, "Where are you bound for? Swinging way over here, I'd say you were trying to get to Arkansas City."

Cullen shook his head. "'No. It wasn't entirely by blind ignorance that we came this way. I have a contract calling for the delivery of this herd at Round Mountain."

"The Pawnee Indian Agency?"

"That's right."

Mike regarded him solemnly, recalling what Ritchie Mc-Christal had told him while drinking. The command of Earl Hollinger, kingpin of the Jayhawkers: no beef for the Round Mountain Pawnees. Jayhawkers already busted two herds this year bound for Round Mountain. Another herd known to be coming up; it wouldn't ever get there. This herd.

"A Jonah outfit on a Jonah trail!" he said at last, and was tempted for a minute to tear up the note. "Sure, I see now why you swung clear over here, trying for a shortcut. I see why you only hired fighters. The Jayhawkers are paying their special attention to any cows bound for Round Mountain. You know it. No herd's made it there this year."

"All the more reason to get my herd through," said Cullen. "D'you know what happens when reservation Indians don't get their promised beef rations?"

"They get hungry. They get sore. And," Mike added cynically, "I know what happens to the price of beef. It goes up."

"They're more than hungry. Starving! And more than sore. The Agent there is scared they'll rise up."

"Somebody should tell him Pawnees are friends to us whites. They've fought on our side against the Cheyennes."

"They're being told that the government has cut off their beef rations—that the ungrateful white man is breaking his promises, lying to them, cheating them." Cullen smacked his fist into the palm of his hand. "In their place, we'd be fighting mad! They are! Don't think they're tame Indians because they've fought on our side and live on a reservation. Those Pawnees are a proud and fierce people."

Mike eyed him curiously, half believing in his sincerity. He said, "That's all very well, but it won't get your herd there. The Jayhawkers all know you're coming up. They're on the lookout for you."

Cullen's eyes frosted in quick suspicion. "How d'you know that?"

"I ran into some fellers who talked about it. That's how well known it is. You still want to push on?"

"You agreed to run the outfit, didn't you?"

"I did, fool that I be."

Critically, Mike watched the herd being bedded down. The men actually did know their work, he decided, but they didn't care how they did it. He'd have to jerk them up damned soon out of that attitude. "Get those wagons out o' there!" he shouted. "Cookee, pull over this way—good flat spot here." Turning to Cullen, he asked, "What's the idea of that big wagon? It's a brute to haul through this kind o' country."

"Needed one with plenty of room," Cullen answered. "It's not as heavy as it looks, and you'll notice it's high slung for good clearance. I traveled from Illinois to Kansas in a wagon like that many years ago, with my brother. We swore by that wagon."

Mike detected a note of nostalgia. "You an Illinois man?"

"I was, till I came West. My brother went on to Colorado and took up mining. I stuck to farming, mostly."

Too bad he hadn't stuck closer, Mike thought, and left this risky game to more experienced heads. The chuck wagon rolled onto the level spot. Mike sent the cook as amiable a nod as he could manage, acknowledging him as a man of top importance in the outfit. The big wagon came on farther, until Cullen motioned to the driver to haul in. The moment it halted, the rear flaps of the canvas top parted and a slim figure sprang lightly down from the tail gate.

Incredulous, aghast, Mike stared at it, from split skirts on up, finally to a pair of dark gray eyes oddly like his own. "God's sake, man!" he burst out at Cullen. "You brought her along! You *did,* blast you!"

CHAPTER SEVEN

The girl stepped up alongside Harley Cullen. She gazed at Mike, her eyes burning. "You again! I saw what you did to Starr, you brute! Is my uncle next? Are you picking a fight with him?"

"No," Mike growled, "But I could turn you over my knee for coming with this crazy outfit! Cullen, don't you know what you've done? Nobody takes a woman along on a trail drive! Don't you know that much? She's a—"

"Watch your language!" Cullen cut in, his square face granite. "Joyce is my niece, my brother's daughter, not whatever it is you may be thinking! She is entitled to—"

"She's a woman, a girl, weeks away from sight of the last one! Entitled to be stared at, talked about! No wonder your scalawag crew slacks off, her on their minds. You can bet they talk and think of nothing else night and day! That's one reason nobody takes a woman along on a trail drive. Just one. There are other reasons I won't go into, which any man knows, or should."

"Any man of your kind, yes." The girl's hot color rose in contrast to the icy scorn of her voice. "The animal kind!"

"I'm surprised you got this far without knowing more about that kind," Mike told her bluntly.

She turned to Cullen. "Why don't you call up the men and have them run him off?"

Cullen stroked his beard. "The fact is, I've engaged him to take Starr's place."

"Oh! I'm sorry to know that."

"You're no sorrier than I am," Mike said. "If I'd known

52

what I know now . . . Cullen, if you can figure any way to send her back—"

"Send her back? Even if it could be done, she has the right to refuse to go. Gould, she's not a child, or a servant, somebody you can bundle off out of the way. I didn't 'bring her along,' as you put it. She chose to come, as she had every right to. Joyce and I are partners in this herd. She's half owner."

"Lord!" Mike swung away and paced a circle. "Lord!" He pulled up short and closed his eyes. "A farmer and a girl—partners in a trail herd! Did you two lose your minds? Did you actually figure you could make it?"

Quietly, the girl retorted, "We still have our herd, Mr. Gould. Where is yours?" Her glance pointedly took in his hard-used appearance.

Cullen had been too full of his own affairs to inquire along that track. He seconded the question, asking in his ignorance, "Did you get through to Abilene? Any trouble from the settlers?"

Mike grimaced, feeling uncomfortably hot and considerably taken down. "Jayhawkers jumped us," he grunted.

His brief reply took a moment to seep in. "D'you mean," Cullen gasped, "you lost your herd?"

"The whole works!"

They fell silent, staring at him, and in their eyes he saw that he stood as a ruined and penniless failure, a man who had fallen to the level of a saddle tramp. Had they showed pity, his temper would have spilled. Perhaps they sensed it. A minute passed before the girl said, "It hardly recommends you to take charge of our herd!"

"The agreement is made, Joyce," said Cullen heavily, looking as if he regretted it. "I've given him a note for two thousand dollars, payable on delivery of the herd at Round Mountain."

"I only hope he earns it!"

Three of the crew came to help Starr over to the chuck wagon, handling him with the casualness of men who were used to the results of bloody brawls. "Gould, here, will give the orders from now on," Cullen told them, none too happily. "He takes Starr's place as trail boss."

They stopped and looked back, inspecting Mike. "Does he, now?" drawled one.

"Yes. Pass the word to the others."

"We will, Mr. Cullen, sir. We sure will. . . ."

The Cullen herd plodded slowly on up rough country that was unmarked by the trails of any previous herds, crossing streams whose names were unknown to Mike. Six miles was a fair day's average, but to try to better that rate was too risky. The cattle were as spooky as wild deer and about as hard to control. Grazing as they traveled, they gained weight. That was all to the good, tending to pacify their nervous belligerence, but the least attempt to push them was apt to bring on a stampede.

The route went by guess, a matter of turning and twisting according to the lay of the land, aiming always in a general northeasterly direction. Cullen spoke of an offshoot of what he called the Tulsa Trail. "I'm not sure where it branches off, but it runs up toward Round Mountain. They say it's passable."

Mike accepted the meager information, marveling that a man knowing so little should tackle so much. "Any trail would look good to me. Hope we strike it somewhere ahead before long."

The crew, bullied by Mike into better order, held their positions, taking more care to make no sudden moves, easing the drifters back into line without upsetting their proddy dispositions. Hostile, resentful, in camp they muttered a lot with Phin Starr, who took no share in the work although his eyes had mended enough for him to see his way about.

After a brief series of flare-up fights the first couple of days, Mike had convinced them that he was running the outfit. They hadn't accepted him, and took his orders silently, glancing toward Starr if he happened to be nearby, deliberately making it plain that they continued to look on Starr as their real boss.

Distrusting them, Mike took to sleeping apart from the camp at night, an hour or two at a time, and lightly at that, with a horse saddled ready to jump on in case of emergency. He grew gaunt and more taciturn, his eyes sunken and steel-sharp. His rags of clothes were giving out, filthy, too sweat-rotted to wash, so that above his chaps he was half naked.

"My uncle and I have been talking about you a good deal," Joyce Cullen remarked to him. She rode alongside him on a buckskin mare, astride-saddle, in her split skirt.

Mike didn't approve of that split skirt. He disliked how the men bulged their eyes, watching for a glimpse of her legs, and exchanged meaning looks. A scalawag crew, for sure. He guessed Phin Starr had recruitted them for Cullen.

There was a lot wrong with this Jonah outfit, not the least being a shapely girl for them to leer at.

He said curtly, "You and your uncle don't know much that's good about me."

"Perhaps there isn't much good to know!"

Nettled by her cool asumption, he took the offensive. "Are you qualified to judge? You or your uncle? I'm a Texas cowman, born of Southern stock. You're the daughter of a Colorado mining man, and your uncle's a Yankee sod-buster. We're that far apart—I'm like a foreigner to you."

She glanced at him. "There's blindness on your side, too. Let me tell you about my uncle. He's more than just a farmer. He founded a settlement near Round Mountain. A farming community, with a little town. It's called Hopewell. He owns the bank there, a very small one."

"All right, he's a farmer-banker." Unimpressed, Mike inquired dryly, "Why didn't he stay with it? The mortgage business is a lot safer than taking a flyer in cattle."

"This is part of it," she answered evenly. "The Hopewell settlers will be the first to suffer if the Round Mountain Pawnees rise. They're nearest, on the edge of the reservation, and there's bad feeling. Lies have been spread, accusing the settlers of plotting to take over Indian lands. The Pawnees are hungry, resentful, desperate."

"Any soldiers stationed at Round Mountain?"

"A small company of infantry, that's all. The authorities won't believe that Pawnees would make war on whites. They don't understand the situation. It's a matter of hunger, of hungry people blaming their neighbors. The Pawnees suspect the settlers of having something to do with cutting off their beef rations. There are more than enough young braves among them to wipe out the garrison and the Hopewell settlement. They're experienced fighters. They've seen service with the army. The settlers are mostly family men, farm folk. Many of them talk of moving out."

"Bad for your uncle's banking business, that!" said Mike. "I see why delivering this herd is so important to him."

"You only think you do!" Joyce Cullen countered. "My uncle feels personally responsible for the Hopewell settlers. He was mainly responsible for having that land opened for settlement, against the opposition of cattlemen who were using it as free range. Cattlemen hate him for that."

"Being a cattleman, I don't wonder! I've never used anything but free and open range."

"He encouraged newcomers and helped them take up homesteads. He helped them get started, helped them through their first lean year or two. What was once range is now good farmland, supporting many families instead of just two or three lordly cattlemen!"

"I've been called this and that," Mike remarked, "but never lordly!"

She ignored it. "Those Hopewell settlers are his people. They look up to him, depend on him, respect—"

"You make him sound more'n a mite lordly, himself."

Pausing to take several breaths, and perhaps counting silently up to ten, she went on. "At the same time, he sympathizes with the Pawnees. Feeding them is the whole problem. Give them their promised beef rations, and their anger will vanish along with their hunger. This herd is the answer," she said, as if Mike might have had difficulty in arriving at that conclusion unaided. "My uncle is far more concerned with saving the Hopewell settlement than he is in making a profit."

Mike nooded, straight-faced, thinking of the difference between six dollars a head purchase price and forty or better on delivery. "And you? He says you're half owner."

"Yes. He found that he couldn't raise enough money to buy the number of cattle he had contracted to deliver. He was required to post a cash bond, and expenses were heavier that he'd calculated. I owned some small mining interests in Colorado, left to me by my father—his brother. He came to me and explained the situation. I've never seen the Hopewell settlement, but he described it, and the people there, and how—"

"And talked you into selling what you had and laying the money on the line with his, eh? All of it?" He shook his head. "In a game neither of you know the first thing about! You don't know how lucky you are that you've got anything to show for it."

Her chin went up. "It's not a game to us. We both put in all we had. He'd turned everything he owned into cash. Even then, to stretch our money he had to search around, finding cheap cattle, beating the price down as much as he could."

"He did that, all right."

A rider came loping back from on forward scout. He was Tanker Todd, a boozy old clown who was said to have cannibal tendencies, but Mike trusted him more than he did any of the others. Todd shouted to Mike, "River ahead—North

Fork, I reckon, an' she's high! I reckon we wait till she drops."

"Another delay!" Joyce Cullen exclaimed. "How long?"

Mike shrugged. "Hard to say. Couple days, maybe—longer if the river keeps rising. Depends on how much rain they've had off up in the hills."

"But we're behind time as it is!"

"I'll go take a look at the river." Passing Todd, Mike said to him, "Cut out that big black steer with the ES brand and bring it up front. Know the one I mean? Belonged to a neighbor of mine, and I happen to know it'll swim."

"You aim to try a crossin'?"

"We'll see. Tell 'em to keep the herd coming, unless I wave to hold off."

The river was steadily rising, Mike saw when he got to it. Tanker Todd's idea of a rise was apt to be exaggerated, he having a prejudice against water in any form, but in this case his report hadn't missed the truth. By tomorrow, Mike estimated, the river would run in full flood, at the rate it was rising. He let the herd come on.

The foremost cattle spread out along the low bank, and others crowded on behind them. After drinking, though, the big black steer balked at taking to the water. This wasn't Lost Creek. This was a river, wide and unfamiliar. The herd continued piling up dangerously in a thickening jam.

Prodded onward, the black steer roared frightened protests, scaring the rest. Mike cursed it. In the next minute or two, half the herd could be lost, the oncoming cattle pushing those stalled on the bank, then the whole bunch winding up tightly in a mad, threshing panic in the river, forcing under and drowning the cows trapped in the middle.

Phin Starr shouted maliciously above the bawling racket, "There goes your herd, Cullen! I never woulda tried this, was I still boss! I got more sense!"

Mike hurriedly stripped off his gun belt and chaps, tugged off his boots, and threw them and his hat to Joyce Cullen. He plunged his horse into the water. Quitting his horse when out in front of the herd, he dodged hoofs and horns and climbed aboard the big black steer.

"Come on, damn you!" he yelled in its ear, pounding it with fists and bare heels. "Get going!" He reached back and twisted its tail.

The astonished steer humped its back and hit the river, and finding deep water it swam strongly. Those already

58 L. L. Foreman

forced belly-high into the river came churning after it, losing some of their senseless terror once the pressure was off them. The herd began loosening out, following the swimmers.

Dropping off the black steer, Mike swam downstream after his horse, in a curve to dodge the cattle. The horse had returned to shore. None of the crew had thought to catch it for him. He caught it at the expense of scratched and stone-bruised bare feet, and rode back up the south bank to where the crew was funneling the herd to the crossing. All hands were not needed for that task. Some were needed on the north bank to line out the cattle as they emerged from the river, and some should have been readying the wagons to float across, but Phin Starr appeared to have taken charge here, or at least he was giving the orders.

As soon as Mike showed up, Harley Cullen blared at him, "Gould, you damn near played hell with the whole herd! What way is that to handle cattle?"

Mike's temper snapped. He was half naked, soaking wet and cold, and his bare feet hurt in the stirrups. What he had done was to risk his life to loosen a disastrous pile-up, and here Cullen was chewing him out as if he had pulled a boner.

"Why, blast your hide!" he rasped. "Don't talk that way to me, you fool sod-buster, or I'll plow you under! Get over there on the other side and line out those cows as they come, before they scatter to hell! Take Starr and some other of your scalawags with you—I sure don't need 'em over here!"

Cullen cooled off, after an affronted stare that won him nothing. He turned his horse to the river. Starr lingered to say, "Some fine day, Texan, you're goin' to—"

"If you've decided to work," Mike broke in on him, "jump to it! With your hands and feet, not your big mouth!"

He watched while Starr motioned to some of the men and rode after Cullen. Finding Joyce sitting her mare behind him, he took his things from her. She scanned his face curiously.

"That was a crazy thing you did, Mike Gould!"

He snapped on his chaps. They were wearing thin at the knees. "Not a bit crazy."

"Reckless, then," she amended.

"Nor reckless." He buckled his gunbelt, sat down to pull on his boots. "Knew what I was doing."

"You could have got yourself gored, or kicked under and drowned, couldn't you?"

"Could've, but I didn't."

"It was the only way to start the cattle across, wasn't it?"

"The only way I could think of right that minute." Cullen's outburst still irritated him, and he said, "You've got more the makings of a cowman than your uncle. Not much *sabe* there."

"Perhaps not. I hardly knew him until we went partners in the herd, but my father always spoke well of him. Why did you take suck a risk?"

He got to his booted feet, slapping on his wreck of a hat. "Now we've got to raft the wagons over. Huh? Why did I do it? Well, for one thing I've got two thousand dollars in that herd."

"You're earning it!"

"Yeah. It's a stake, and I need it. It means a lot to me."

She said quietly, "Money means a good deal to me, too. For a man, poverty is a misfortune that can be remedied. For a girl, it's a calamity that strips her of her independence. I own nothing outside of my share of the cattle. That's not altogether what bothers me, though."

Mike made to leave, but she detained him by saying, "If we don't get the cattle to Round Mountain in time, and the Pawnees rise, a lot of people will suffer—men, women and children. So will the Pawnees suffer, when the army goes after them. Were you thinking of that?"

"No," he disclaimed curtly. "I just don't like to be broke, is all. I've been there."

He swung onto his horse while raising his voice in a harsh yell at some of the men. "Go easy, there—don't push 'em! Couple of you cross over downstream to pick up drifters. Current's pretty strong." Under his breath he muttered, "Goddam Arbuckle outfit!"

Joyce spoke behind him. "Aren't you hard on them?"

"Am I easy on myself?" he retorted. He heeled his horse on down to the river's edge, and hailed, "Cullen, line 'em out north soon's you get over. Keep 'em moving. I'll see to the wagons." Dryly, he queried, "You remember which way is north?"

Swimming the river on his horse, Harley Cullen looked back and nooded solemnly. Their idea of establishing north, Mike had learned, was to set the tongue of the chuck wagon aimed at the North Star in the evening, and draw a point from it the next morning. The system was workable only if some fool didn't sit on the wagon tongue and jiggle it, or blunder into it in the dark, fall over it and kick it out of kilter. Next morning, north was apt to be northeast, northwest, any old direction yonderly. It could go toward explaining how the outfit had got itself lost.

True, Cullen insisted that he had bent northeasterly on purpose, as a shortcut to Round Mountain, and in order to shun the regular routes. Although he was prepared for Jayhawkers, or fancied he was, he preferred avoiding them if he could, especially as he had his niece along.

But he had angled off too soon and too far into untracked country, with all the confidence of Moses in the wilderness. Phin Starr should have known better than to let him do it. Any of the crew should have realized what the outfit was getting into. Yet apparently nobody had raised an argument. On the contrary, they had all slouched along, not a care in the world, as if they actually knew where they were going. That was hard to understand.

CHAPTER EIGHT

Although Harley Cullen didn't go so far as to apologize for his outburst, he did unbend enough to tell Mike that he was satisfied with the handling of the herd. Mike took the modest compliment without comment.

Shifting to the subject of Jayhawker raiders, Cullen remarked somewhat smugly, "That's one trouble I managed to avoid!"

His implication was plain: he had outsmarted the dreaded Jayhawkers, while Mike had lost his herd to them. A farmer-banker had proved himself more competent than experienced Texas trail drivers. In his self-congratulation he was blandly leaving out of account the fact that he had gone hopelessly astray—that only by working himself to skin and bone had Mike got him out of that jackpot.

Mike let it pass, only saying, "We're not there yet."

They had struck a trail that Cullen promptly decided must be the one he had spoken of, the offshoot from the Tulsa Trail, leading them up toward Round Mountain. He considered it the last long lap, the easiest part of the whole trip. The closer he progressed toward his home grounds, the more autocratic he became, Mike noticed. He issued orders like a hard-nosed colonel.

"The herd's strung out too far! Tighten up, there! See to it, Gould! . . ."

He cloaked himself in dignity, the big man of Hopewell coming home in triumph to save the day. No doubt he deserved credit for all that he had done and was doing for the rosy-named farming settlement that he had founded. He had staked all he owned for the benefit of his people.

61

Very much his people. His subjects, ever beholden to him. Mike speculated as to how high Cullen's personal popularity stood among those Hopewell settlers. Bossiness wasn't an endearing trait, nor vanity. At this rate, by the time he arrived home he'd be ten feet tall.

In response to Mike's short comment, Cullen declared with authority, "We're as good as there, far as Jayhawkers are concerned! To my knowledge they're never seen over in these parts. They prowl the main trails, watching for Texas herds. I'm surprised you Texans don't do as I did! Matter of habit, I suppose. Some people can't change. Not quite enough, ah, initiative!"

"I guess our ways suit us."

"Fortunately, the damn' Jayhawkers stick to their settled ways, too! I counted on that, of course."

"Your counting's a little off, there," Mike said. He gave him the information that he had gained from Ritchie McChristal.

"So they're organized now? All the Jayhawker bands?" Cullen shook his head. "I didn't know that."

"Neither did I. I doubt it's much known as yet, outside of themselves. They recruit fresh blood, but they're mighty careful who they take in. They're getting bigger, spreading out, so let's don't be too sure they're all prowling the main trails! The order's gone out to them to bust this herd, as I told you!"

A flicker of anxiety returned to Cullen's eyes. "You make them sound like an army!"

"That's what they are!" Mike said. "An army of badmen! For all I know, they're about to turn the Territory into a robbers' roost, or as much of it as they can control. Their kingpin has worked out a smart system for selling stolen cattle under his own brands. He's a cattleman, Hollinger by name. Owns a ranch on the Kansas line, and another somewhere down here in the Territory."

Cullen stared fixedly at him. "Hollinger? Is his first name Earl?"

"Right. Friend of yours?"

"No!" Cullen uttered the word explosively. "Earl Hollinger headed the cattlemen's group that fought to keep the Hopewell country from being opened for settlers. His friends gave up, finally, after I got court orders and injunctions against them. Not Hollinger! He sent night-riders to terrorize my people. He tried to have me murdered. As perhaps you've guessed, I don't like cattlemen! They're bad losers!"

"I won't argue that point."

The concession won only a snort. "I know about Hollinger's Kansas ranch, of course. He runs a dozen brands or more. But since when did he start a ranch down here?"

Mike shook his head. "Couldn't say. What kind of a party is he?"

"He's the kind of cattleman I most despise!" Cullen stated forcefully. "An overbearing bully, arrogant, intolerant, who thinks he has the right to claim all the range he wants, regardless of other people's rights! Hates all settlers, and to him the only good Indian is a dead Indian. Do you recognize the breed? You should!"

"I've met a few here and there," Mike granted. "With all their faults, though, they don't generally go in for wholesale robbery and murder."

"They draw the line at nothing! You being a cattleman, you're only speaking in defense of—"

"I'm not defending anybody. I'm saying Hollinger's pulling the biggest cattle-steal I ever heard of!"

"He's typical of his breed!"

"We better drop this," Mike said, and changed the subject. "Ought to be coming to the Cimarron soon. Guess I'll ride on a ways."

He could take just so much of Cullen and his increasingly opinionated high-and-mightiness. No wonder Cullen had made bitter enemies of the ranchers who had once used the Hopewell country. You couldn't make friends of ranchers by turning their best range into homesteads, but at least you could try to be a little diplomatic. In his sweeping denunciation of cattlemen, Cullen displayed as much arrogant intolerance as any of them.

For the rest of that day Mike rode alone well in advance of the herd, preferring his own company. Recent signs of cattle caused him to question if this really was the offshoot trail to Round Mountain. If so, then somebody had passed this way with a bunch of cows lately, ahead of Cullen. No wagon tracks. Maybe it was another trail that Cullen didn't know about, meandering off into cow country, and that bunch of cows was being moved to new range. Whatever it was, it had to strike the Cimarron somewhere.

In the wane of afternoon he sighted a long bend of the Cimarron, glistening like gold under the sinking sun. The trail lined onward to meet it, and he saw where it continued on the far side. It was too late to make the crossing today. He turned back and located a bedding ground for the night.

When the herd came up, he saw by the men's faces that their tempers were ugly. The cause soon became clear. Cullen, hauling on his sweating horse in his clumsily heavy-handed fashion, blared to him, "They keep letting the herd string out too far!"

"And you've been raking 'em for it," Mike said.

"Certainly! I pay their wages! You've raked them mighty free, haven't you?"

"I do it different. They hate my guts, but they take it. From you, no. You've got your horse in a lather, and yourself too!"

Cullen hit the horn of his saddle with his fist. "I've had to ride up and down the herd, doing your job while you——"

"I took a scout," Mike interrupted.

"There's no need scouting a plain trail! From now on, Gould, you stay on your job, hear?" Cullen cast a look at the sun. "We've got another hour or more of daylight. Why are we stopping?"

Mike held his temper. Somebody in the outfit had to keep his head. "The Cimarron's a couple miles on, and I don't figure to push on near it in the dark. I picked this spot so's we'll get the herd strung out ready to cross in the morning. Clear to you?"

Cullen rolled his shoulders, grunted, stared sternly at the cattle filing onto the bedding ground. "Well, now that we've halted, I suppose . . ."

"Yeah. I hope the cook'll fix something fit to eat. It might set up your boogery crew to where they won't crave to cut our heads off."

By making an early start, they began the crossing before the sun rose high enough to strike the water and spook the leaders. The Cimarron had a bad name, and Mike expected a bobble or two. He watched with growing satisfaction as the long column dipped and went streaming across. But there Harley Cullen ended his inept venture in cattle.

Joyce Cullen saw it, and she called out urgently, pointing. Mike looked in time to see Cullen go under. Cullen and Phin Starr and two of the crew were swimming their horses over on the upstream side of the crossing herd. Cullen was near-est to the splashing column. Something either startled his horse, or else the current in mid-channel caught him unprepared, for he and his struggling horse drifted right into the ruck of cattle.

A horseman in the water was nowhere near as authoritative to cattle as a horseman tall in the saddle on solid ground. Cullen promptly disappeared under water, all but his hat, when a swimming steer rammed his horse and then got the notion to climb onto the saddle with him. The panicked horse came up without him, rolling and kicking, nearly causing a mill in midstream.

They fished him out, a quarter-mile down the river. A steer had hoofed him over the eyes and knocked him senseless, and he bore other marks of abuse, any of which could have disabled him from swimming well even had he been a good swimmer. It was the air trapped under his hard-weave cloth coat and baggy trousers that finally floated him to the surface in calmer water. He was dead, either from drowning, injuries, or both.

Nobody in the outfit had a Bible. In a Texas outfit somebody would likely have owned a prayer book tucked away in his warbag if only for luck. Not these men. Joyce said she had one packed in the big wagon, but a quick search failed to turn it up and there wasn't time to ramsack all the contents of that ill-chosen vehicle.

They dug him a decent grave, though, and having buried him they laid rocks over it against the coyotes. When it was done, Mike bared his head and said as a last service, "He was a good man where he belonged, I reckon, and did good to a lot of folks there. He didn't belong on a trail drive—not this kind. God forgive all his mistakes and rest his soul. Amen."

He crammed his hat back on his head. "Let's get after the cows."

Joyce waited until evening to speak to him, when the herd was bedded down and the cook's fires glowed in the dusk. "You're hard and callous!" she accused him. "Was it his fault that he knew so little about trail driving? He wasn't a Texas cattleman. He was a farmer, a banker, the founder of a thriving settlement. He never wanted to be any kind of cattleman!"

She was not pretending to being broken up by her uncle's death. Too honest for false grief. She hadn't known him well or for very long. Mike guessed that she and Harley Cullen hadn't hit it off any too smoothly, under the surface. They weren't much alike. Their backgrounds were different, and where Cullen had retained intact his preconceived opinions, she had gathered knowledge and understanding of the problems of trailing a herd.

"I didn't mean it like that," Mike answered, getting hot coffee for her from the huge, blackened pot. "I spoke what lay in my mind, the truth as I saw it and as I still see it. A good man can make mistakes. His worst mistake was setting out with a herd in the first place without one real working cowman in the crew. These are scum! Throw—offs! Barroom badmen and brush-dodgers!"

All day he had picked at a suspicion that Cullen's death wasn't as accidental as it appeared. That horse he'd ridden, a placid plug, stolid as a preacher's Sunday mount, didn't startle easily. Phin Starr had been close by him, and those other two. An unseen spur, under water, raked hard at the plug's belly, could have done it. A malicious impulse, perhaps. Rancor; revenge for Cullen's rough tongue yesterday.

He didn't speak to Joyce of his suspicion. He said to her, "Cullen's gone. I guess that leaves you full owner of the herd, if there's no closer kin. In any case, you stand as the owner till we make delivery."

"When my uncle and I went into partnership, we made out our wills in each other's favor as far as the herd is concerned. It was a business arrangement for our mutual protection."

Mike swallowed bitter coffee tasting of ashes and a pot never scoured. "Cook should wash his socks in the dishpan. All right, now I'll speak my mind to you. I boss your outfit the rest of the way, deliver at Round Mountain, and collect my two thousand dollars. Boss, you hear? You're owner, but I give all orders."

"Agreed!" she snapped, nettled by his tone.

"Let's get it straight. It means if I tell you to get in your wagon, you jump to it, no argument!"

She flushed, raising her chin. "Was this how you lost your herd? By bullying everyone around you?"

He looked at her impassively. "How I lost my herd is between me and the Jayhawkers. I don't aim to lose this one. I've never seen Pawnees break out, but I'd imagine they—" He cut himself off. "Lady, I'm a tired and hungry man. Finish your plate and don't rile me!"

"Yes, sir!"

"Early start tomorrow—"

"Yes, sir!"

"So get to bed early."

"Yes, *sir!*" she said between her teeth. "Right now!"

She set down her plate and mug for him to carry to the wreck-pan. He wiped off the beginnings of a grin, and watched her march off to the big wagon.

His thoughts strayed to the half-opinion that he had first formed about her, back on Lost Creek—that she was a high-class doxy selling her expensive company to Harley Cullen, passing off as his niece. He had guessed wrong there on every count, and owed her an apology and himself a swift kick. But she certainly was plenty attractive enough to give rise to his error.

And it might have been better had she been one, he mused. That kind was simpler to deal with, on the whole. More tractable. Less likely to seethe and blow up for purely personal reasons. He would have to use a short rein on Joyce, or she could become a worse problem than she was already. She had a lively temper.

He yawned, got up, and carried the dishes to the cook's wreck-pan, listening automatically to the monotonous, unmusical warbling of the two men riding night guard on the herd. Phin Starr stood talking in low tones to the cook and Tanker Todd. The rest of the crew sat around the cook's fire, silent as a ring of waiting buzzards. No amiable hoorawing in this outfit.

"Early start in the morning," Mike told them.

"Couldn't make it too early for me," Starr said, and moved off.

Mike looked after him, mildly puzzled by his remark. Such willingness was unlike Starr. Glancing at the men around the fire, Mike got an impression that one was missing. He counted heads, scanned them more slowly, and asked, "Where's that feller in the beaver hat?" The name came to him and he spoke it. "Burke."

Burke acted and looked more like a broken-down tinhorn gambler than a cowman. In any other outfit Mike wouldn't have thought to inquire after him or any other hand. A man had the right to solitude on his own time when and if he wanted it.

Nobody volunteered a reply, nor raised eyes from the fire Mike had to repeat his question twice, before one of the men said, "He rid back lookin' for a slicker he dropped."

"In the dark?"

"It's a yaller slicker, He'll find it."

Mike conjured up a mental picture of the missing Burke, and found no yellow slicker in it. "I didn't know he had one."

"That ain't all you don't know!" said the man.

Mike fixed a stare on him, but the man kept his eyes down. "Just how'd you mean that?"

From the darkness, Starr rasped surprisingly, "Button your lip, Max, it's the boss you're talkin' to!" And in a quieter tone—"Pay no 'tention, Gould, they're just sick o' this drive an' want it over. I'll have 'em on tap early, don't you worry!"

Mike dug out his bedroll—two blankets and a tarp, borrowed from the Cullen wagon. He carried it to the wagon and crawled underneath. Why he chose that spot on this particular night, he wasn't sure, except that a sense of wrongness troubled him, and common loyalty to the herd's owner demanded that he stick close by.

He lay examining three circumstances. The missing Burke, off searching in the dark for a lost slicker. If he owned a yellow slicker, he hadn't carried it rolled and tied behind his saddle where it might have worked loose and fallen off unbeknownst to him. He hadn't worn it during rains.

Mike frowned. " He got as soaked as I did!"

The man at the fire had lied, then, but possibly he had lied for no other reason than sheer orneriness. His cryptic retort, that last remark he'd made, could have had hidden meaning or none at all—a surly barb aimed offhand at the hated boss.

Phin Starr's sudden change of attitude . . . he still held the crew in the palm of his hand, no question about that. He had constantly egged them on to acts of sly insolence, masked insults, perverse cussedness disguised as misunderstanding. Tonight he had switched sides and bawled out a man. Perhaps, the drive nearing its end, he . . .

"Mike, are you awake?"

The voice came from above him. Joyce's voice. He guessed she was speaking down from the rear end of the wagon.

"Yes," he answered her. "Anything wrong?"

"No," she said quickly. "Are you worried?"

"No," he lied.

"Then why are you awake?"

Feminine logic, he supposed, was involved in that question. Or feminine intuition. How had she known he was lying here with his eyes wide open? He started to say that he was awake because he wasn't asleep, but instead said, "I was thinking about things. You better get to sleep."

"Yes, sir. You too!"

"Yes, ma'am."

"Good night."

"Good night."

CHAPTER NINE

Seven men, well mounted and heavily armed with six-guns and rifles, waited on the trail in the mid-morning sunshine. One of them, a blond giant with protruding blue eyes, raised an imperious hand as if commanding every living thing in the oncoming Cullen herd to halt dead in its tracks forthwith.

Mike, riding ahead, came up to the seven. Their faces spelled trouble, telling him that his sense of wrongness last night was founded on more than a thin premonition. Receiving no greeting, and offering none, he said to them, "Well?"

The blond man ran a deliberate survey over him, as he might have inspected someone known unfavorably to him by hearsay. "My name is Hollinger," he announced, and watched Mike's face for a reaction. His tone and manner conveyed a confident expectation of respect, deference, if not outright fear. "You're crossing my range!"

Wanting to call him a liar, Mike asked, "You lease it from the Indians?"

"I don't make deals with vermin! My range is anywhere my cattle graze!"

Coming from any other man, Mike would have put that broad statement down to sheer bombast. But this was the mighty Hollinger, head of the Jayhawkers, the brain that had welded the roving bands into an organized legion under his iron control. He meant what he said, in dead earnest. Cullen hadn't half-stated the case, describing Hollinger as an arrogant and intolerant cattleman of the worst type. He belonged to a past era of cattle barons who grabbed all the land from horizon to horizon, and killed off all contenders, red or

70

white. In this age he was a fanatic, dangerous as an avalanche.

"We'll cut your herd for strays!"

As a request it would have been reasonable, discussed with courtesy on both sides. This came as a flat demand. "We haven't picked up any strays," Mike said.

Hollinger motioned at a dark man fingering a rawhide riata. "This is Lew Keeley, my range boss. He'll handle it."

Mike hunched over in his saddle. He looked at Lew Keeley's riata, knowing it for a California kind of throwing-rope, four strands of rawhide braided tight and hard, greased, patiently worked so pliable that in expert hands it appeared to have a life of its own. Lew Kelley's rig, too, bespoke country west of the Rockies, so he most likely could use that long riata. Centerfire saddle, high fork and cantle, full stamped and prettied up with silver conchas. Silver spurs. Eagle-bill tapaderos.

"My name's Mike Gould." He stuck a thumb over his shoulder. "That's the Cullen herd coming up this free and open trail. I'm the trail boss, and I'll see you to hell before you chouse those cows! You can pull off and check brands as they go by. You don't cut!"

Hollinger nodded to his range boss. "We cut!" The armed squad quietly spread out in line abreast, blocking the trail.

Lew Keeley gazed with chill thoughtfulness at Mike, while shaking out the loop of his coiled riata. He waited until the leading steers came up. He fastened his eyes on the big black steer, which had decided that it was number one since the North Fork crossing. Phin Starr, arriving with the point riders, looked at Hollinger and reined aside. The point riders did the same.

"One of ours, that, I'd say," Kelley murmured, blandly disregarding the plain ES brand as well as the road brand. "Let's have a look at it." The riata snaked forward.

To cut a herd without permission was intolerable enough, but roping down the lead steer put the cap on it. Mike acted fast, seeing what was coming. His short maguey rope sailed out and slapped across Keeley's riata, spoiling the throw. While the big black steer ambled untroubledly by, Mike said, "Dally-man, don't you try that again!"

He was one against seven, and he glanced around to see if the crew was coming up to help out. In any kind of outfit he had ever known, good and bad, all hands backed the trail boss against outsiders, regardless of private feuds and personal dislike. But Phin Starr and the others were holding off, and he saw no prospect of their pitching in. There was scant difference between their expressions and those of the Hollinger squad. Their eyes, fixed on him, held much the same look of coldly hostile expectancy. They took the place of witnesses to a thoroughly approved execution.

It flashed through his mind again that Starr had been close by when Cullen's horse lunged off on that crazy tangent and got snarled up among the swimming cattle. The reaching jab of a sharpened and locked spur rowel . . . Starr wore wired spurs, the rowels the size of silver dollars.

And Burke, gone all night, showing up this morning, shaking his head blankly when asked if he had found his lost slicker. The man at the fire: *"That ain't all you don't know!"* Starr had shut him up.

It came to Mike bleakly that he was alone, trapped into a prepared deadfall, nobody to back him—except Joyce Cullen, riding hard up the column of plodding cattle, a rifle swinging in her right hand. She screamed to him "Watch out!"

He jerked around, barely in time to see Lew Keeley's rawhide riata whirling for his head.

It was a straight throw, a hungry loop designed to snub fast, yank him off saddle, and drag him over rocks and through the brush. He had seen that done, in a deadly riata duel between two fiery vaqueros whose rage at each other could not be satisfied by gunshots. The loser ended as a bloody hulk, stripped naked and torn to the bones.

He was riding the grulla. He bent over, the saddle horn punching his chest, and dug in his heels. The horse leaped like a scalded cat, and the rawhide loop slapped Mike's back and slid off its flank. Mike reined around, glaring.

Unperturbed by his first miss, Keeley deftly gathered up his fifty-foot line, smiling, whipping it into coils with the rapid grace of an expert roper. His eyes mutely challenged Mike. He was out to make sport and display his skill.

Mike carried a thirty-five-foot maguey rope, made of the tough fiber of century plants, hard-twisted, tied fast to his saddle horn. A Texas rope. Keeley's glance touched it contemptuously. California-style ropers scorned the short maguey and the double-cinched saddle of tie-fast men—the rig fashioned for working in thick Texas brush where a long rope wasn't much good; where a man rode in close to dab on his loop, had no time to take a dally around his saddle horn, and didn't figure to let the critter get away whatever else happened.

Mike rode at Keeley, picking up the challenge, knowing it had to be that or a shoot-out next minute. Lacking Keeley's reach of fifty feet, he needed to get in at closer quarters.

They looked on, Hollinger's squad and the Cullen crew. And Joyce Cullen. She uttered no sound now. Mike caught a flash of her white face, her dismayed eyes.

Lew Keeley darted his horse aside, spun it around on a light neck-rein, and twirled a loop, still smiling his taunting, contemptuous smile. He rode superbly, the kind of man who did all things so well that he afforded himself flourishes of lithe grace. The riata flicked, the whippy rawhide whispering through its smooth white bone honda. His loop folded into a *mangana de cabra,* neat and tricky, a curling figure eight designed to snap onto Mike's neck and the neck of the grulla at the same instant. Mike dodged it by inches, but his own loop went to pot. Keeley laughed aloud, circling his horse and winding up again, making it known by his laugh that he relished playing a cat-and-mouse game with his victim.

The next lightning throw was a hoolihan, flipped backward in one swing, the wide loop closing and flattening out to ring the target at the full length of the rope. Mike rode right into it. He hit the grulla's head down with his fist, and ducked low. He used his left fist, his right hand busy with the short maguey. His knee and heel commanded the grulla to switch end-for-end, scattering dirt in a tight turn, and he rode again at Keeley, onto the dragging riata in hopes of hoof-cutting it.

Anxious to save his precious rawhide riata from being stepped on and ruined, Keeley gave it a mighty twitch that brought it lashing back to him. Lacking the time to coil it up and build another loop before Mike could reach him, he slung his horse half around to jump out of range. For that brief moment he lost his perfect control of the riata; it loosely slapped his horse's hind legs, and the horse shied.

The maguey rope settled over him from behind. A straight toss, no whirl to give him an instant's warning, the loop snapped his arms snug to his body. His horse ran on. The tightened rope plucked him backward out of the saddle and slammed him to the ground.

The cow-wise grulla halted at once, legs braced, holding the rope taut for Mike to hog-tie and brand the caught critter. Mike touched it to a sidling shuffle, dragging Keeley, who cursed while trying to free his arms from the rope.

"Want that noose to slip up round your neck?" Mike asked him. "It's all right with me. I'll give you a little slack to help, you say so!"

Keeley didn't say so, appearing to consider it a doubtful choice between strangling and getting towed over rocks at full gallop. He stopped struggling, and stared toward the Hollinger squad, his eyes silently begging for help.

Hollinger rapped, "Turn him loose, Gould!"

Mike let the grulla take another sidling step that dragged Keeley that much closer to a patch of thornbush. "Would he have turned me loose if he'd downed me?"

"That's—"

"Would you've told him to?"

"That's nothing to do with what I'm telling you! Turn him loose right now!"

"Go to hell! Any of you make a move, I'll slip the rope and jerk his head off!" Mike held onto the rope, ready to heel the grulla to a flying start. "I think I'll keep him till we get past your stamping ground. Then you can have him."

"You fool! Do you think you can buck me?" Hollinger made a staying gesture at his riders. "Wait, I'll see if I can talk some sense into him! What are you trying to do, Gould?"

"Get this herd to Round Mountain."

"Why? What's in it for you to feed Indians? It's not your herd. What difference if Indians starve?"

"The difference," Mike answered," is they're likely to jump the Hopewell folks, and you know it!"

"Settlers!" Hollinger spat. He shook his blond head in genuine anger and disgust. "Vermin, like the Indians! Time and again I warned them to get out of that cow country, to get off my range and stay off! You're a cattleman—you ought to be on my side, not theirs. Damn them, let the Indians jump them!"

"You're doing all you can to bring it on!"

"It's their own choice! Let them see blood, they'll run! The army can clean it up, kill off a few hundred Indians—"

"And soon's it's all over," Mike broke in, "you'll take back that range. Sure. With official blessing. It'll be said that settlers make for trouble when they're too close to an Indian reservation, but big cattlemen like you can handle Indians. Know how to keep 'em in their place."

"You're seeing the light, Gould!" Hollinger said.

Mike nodded. "I see it. So lay off this herd, or you'll be needing a new range boss!" He pulled on his rope and made some slack. Keeley instinctively spread his pinned arms as the pressure loosened. Mike gave the rope a quick flip and a tug that drew the noose up around Keeley's neck. He tugged it again, warningly. Keeley gasped.

Hollinger opened his mouth to speak, but it was Joyce who called, "Hold it, Mike! Hold it!"

They all looked at her. She held the rifle raised, staring northward up the trail. Mike followed the direction of her eyes. His baleful anger abruptly lost its edge. He loosened his choking rope on Keeley, and said to Hollinger, "Take him!"

To Joyce he said, "Easy with that rifle! Put it down!"

Hollinger gave the nod, his prominent blue eyes at once irate and cautious. Swiftly, his armed squad pulled Keeley upright and helped him onto his horse. Casting glances up the trail, they took to the brush.

Hollinger, last to leave, called back harshly, "See you another time, Gould!" As he put his horse to a canter, he added, "Maybe!"

"Maybe!" Mike echoed, and surveyed the mob of riders that had suddenly and silently ghosted up on the trail.

He estimated upwards of sixty of them. They huddled in shabby blankets, bits of castoff army uniform, worn-out buckskins and shreds of shirts, yet the sight of them had sent kingly Hollinger and his picked squad heading for distance. They sat their scrawny little ponies in careless disorder. The only bright color about them was in the dyed eagle feathers stuck into their black hair. No war paint, but the feathers were red-tipped. The strong, hard faces needed no paint to touch up their dangerous ferocity.

Mike said again to Joyce, "Put that rifle down! Put it away, you hear? If I was them I wouldn't want to see it pointed my way. I'd be inclined to do something about it!"

These coppery apparitions were men who paid homage to nobody, willingly, and they didn't know the meaning of humility. Quick to grin or scowl. As sensitive in their battered pride as any Spanish grandees. Gods of the earth, in their own opinion. Able fighters, scouts, trackers. No weapons showed among them, except knives, but the shabby blankets could conceal much more than lean bodies.

They traveled without women and children, without pack animals or even a single travois. All men. A bad sign. They were poor, and their memories of better days fed dark discontent. Broken promises. Their sense of injustice could spark into berserk rage.

Phin Starr and the crew were backing off, at the point of taking flight and abandoning the herd. They moved with slow care, in fear that any sudden action would trigger the silent mob to a howling charge. Mike barked at them, "Stand tight! If they come at us you won't get far!"

Joyce said to him, "But you can't fight them off!"

"No. Don't aim to try." He handed her his gun and rode on forward at a walk.

He had known Indians here and there, had dealings with some, and on the whole had got along with them when the conditions permitted. There was in him a good deal of their forthright view of things, as well as an occasional turn for dry humor that they could appreciate.

He picked out the leader, an ancient hawk of a man in the forefront, tall and cavernous-eyed. Hand raised in greeting, he nodded to him. Pulling out his tobacco sack, he offered it. The sack contained the last of his tobacco, and it wasn't much to offer, but he made a small ceremony of the courtesy, a prelude to friendly gabbing.

The sunken black eyes regarded him impassively. They made him feel that perhaps he should have headed in some other direction for his health. The mob stayed motionless. Slowly, then, a thin brown hand emerged from under the leader's blanket. Palm up, it acknowledged his greeting briefly, grudgingly. It ignored the tobacco sack completely— a blunt intimation to him that an understanding was not to be bought so easily.

Cheap congeniality was worthless to hungry men, and these men looked famished. Mike realized that they had come through tough times and were out of patience.

From the wrinkled old lips dropped one word, uttered in bitter mockery like a request flung over a cocked gun: *"Wohaw!"*

Not begging. A demand. They wanted *wohaw* and they would have it—beef. Good red meat to roast, to fill their shrunken stomachs, for nourishment and strength. Men's food. They were desperate for it.

And Mike, disregarding the fact that he had stood off Hollinger's demand, compromised with this one. The old chief wore a silver ring on his finger, the only visible article of any value on his person, and it worth no more than a dollar or two. Mike pointed to it, then toward the cattle. He held up three fingers and went into sign language. Three fat steers for the silver ring. Or no deal, nothing. He was not to be pushed around.

The cavernous black eyes kindled understandingly. Here was a man of sense and self-respect. The old chief slid the silver ring off, presented it to Mike, and the deal was made, dignity sustained on both sides. The eyes of the mob glistened. Lips worked in anticipation of the feast to come.

Mike yelled back to the crew, "Cut out three fat steers for my friend here! He's bought 'em for his commissary department."

He watched the mob of Indians go swarming off, driving the three doomed steers before them. The old chief rode back to him and said in perfectly clear English, "I am Sakuruta. You?"

"Mike Gould."

"Your beef will taste sweet to us, Mike Gould. I hope you make better trade with the rest of your cows!" With that he loped off to rejoin his warriors.

Mike grinned after him. Cagey old devil, playing the blanket Indian, sign language and all, when he could parley in English with anybody. He lifted his voice to the crew. "All right, trim up the herd and let's mosey on!"

Joyce said to him later in the day, "You're inconsistent!"

"How's that?"

"Hollinger only wanted to cut the herd for strays. You refused to let him. You fought his man. I think you'd have killed him, if the Indians hadn't come when they did."

"You can be dead sure he'd have killed me, give him the chance!"

"But then you gave in to the Indians. That ring isn't worth anything. You let them take what they wanted, pretending it was a trade!"

"Yeah," he agreed, gazing at the silver ring on his little finger. "I sure got rooked on the trade. But they were starving, you see. If I'd given 'em the beef for nothing they'd figure this was a miserable kind of outfit they could rob how they liked. Which it sure is, far as the crew's concerned! Your uncle was a poor picker of—"

"Must you speak ill of the dead?"

He shrugged, doubtful that death should remove a man from an honest opinion of his actions in life. "If I'd refused the beef to those Indians," he continued, "they'd have dealt us grief. So I made a trade of it. They went off happy, and we're on our way. Seems simple to me, don't know about you!"

Irritated by his casual assumption of superior wisdom, she said, "You made the trade, as you call it, without consulting me! Not a word!"

"Wasn't it understood I boss this outfit?"

"That doesn't give you permission to act like the owner of the herd!" she insisted. "Those cows you made so free with were mine, not yours!"

His gaze turned stony. "Hell!" he drawled, using the swear-word deliberately. "Sounds like you care more about the dollars than even I do! All right, Miss Owner, you can take the price of three cows out of my pay when we make delivery! Satisfy you?"

"I didn't mean—"

"Charge up what I eat, too, while you're at it!"

He booted his horse and left her with that insult, not seeing her shamed flush, her small white teeth biting her lower lip, the tears starting in her eyes.

In his mind sprang the thought that they were too much alike in some ways, he and she, for them to hit it off. Supposedly, like attracted like; actually, it could cause friction. He cursed the visions that were making his scant sleeping hours restless of late. Damn it, he was getting as bad as the crew, missing no chance to catch her eye, to exchange a word with her.

Hell take all that. She just happened to be the one and only female around in an all-too-masculine environment, and any fool could predict the result. She being the owner of the herd didn't help matters. He decided henceforth to steer clear of her company, avoid meeting her eyes, and to speak to her only when it was absolutely necessary.

CHAPTER TEN

Toward sundown a lone rider showed up, coming from the north. He was a knotty little man whose hard gray eyes looked younger than his graying hair. His name, he told Mike, was Thad Meserve. He flashed a small badge.

"United States marshal."

Mike stiffened warily. "On business?" Reflecting upon a few irregularities of his past, he withheld his name for the time being.

Meserve nodded. "Trailing a band of Pawnees. Maybe you've seen 'em. They're led by a chief named Sakuruta. Tall, skinny, old as the hills. Name means Coming Sun, but his sun'll sink if he pulls anything before I catch up with him!"

Noncommital, Mike said, "This is the Cullen herd. I'm Mike Gould, the trail boss. We're bound for Round Mountain."

"That's where the Sakuruta band comes from. We don't know what they're up to." Meserve's restless glance swept over Mike's dilapidated garb, his gun, his hands. "Trouble's brewing up there. If it boils over, God help the Hopewell settlers! They'll catch hell before help can reach 'em. Cullen, you said? Harley Cullen, of Hopewell?"

"Yeah. He's dead."

"Sorry to hear it. He had enemies who'll be glad. One, especially"

"Earl Hollinger, you mean," Mike said. "He already knows."

The marshal quirked an eyebrow. "You've met him?"

"He tried to give me trouble."

"I'd be surprised if he didn't! All respect to cattlemen,

but some of 'em get too big. Hollinger wouldn't be satisfied to own the whole Territory, and Kansas thrown in. I can't prove he's got a hand in the Round Mountain trouble." He eyed Mike estimatingly. "Can you? How much do you know?"

Mike shook his head. "Proof, no. Hearsay, yes, plenty."

"And you're keeping it to yourself. That's no help to me."

"After I get this herd delivered, I'll give you all the help you want. It'll keep till then. I lost my own herd. Like you, I can't prove Hollinger was behind it. I'm just damn sure he was!"

An old impatience bunched the muscles of Meserve's jaw. "You cattlemen wouldn't give the law the time of day, only when it suits you!" he charged. "These Pawnees I'm trailing, they're all warriors. Sakuruta is a war chief. They quit the reservation without notice. The Indian Agent at Round Mountain raised the alarm."

"He lose his head?" Mike asked.

"He knows it's a touchy situation. My job is to talk 'em into going back before harm's done. If I can't, it's a job for the army, which I'd hate to see. Could start a general Pawnee revolt. Sakuruta's got big prestige. First I have to find him."

"Would he listen to you?"

"My mother was a Pawnee," Meserve mentioned simply. "It got me this job. I've told you about it so you'll know I'm not out to arrest Sakuruta or trick him to jail. I want to keep the peace, what's left of it. You're wearing his ring! Kindly answer one straight question, forgetting for this once you're a close-mouthed brush-buster with no respect for law officers! Where are my Pawnees?"

Mike grinned, unoffended. "They're back a ways down off the trail, eating beef lawfully traded for. If I'd known they came from right where we're going, I'd have got a receipt payable by the Agent."

"I hope to God you get there!" Meserve assured him. "More and more, the Pawnees believe they're being cheated. They've had two or three crooked Agents who got rich off them. They're saying the Great White Father"—he grimaced —"has disowned his red sons and daughters. Turned his back on the warriors who've never failed to fight on his side against the hostile tribes. I'm red and white, and I'll say there's considerable truth in it! Between campaigns the Pawnees get a lean deal, while captured hostiles fare better!"

"It's the screeching wheel that gets the grease, eh?"

"And they're about to screech! Ever see Pawnees on the whoop? You missed something! I was an army scout." Meserve chewed his lip reflectively. "If I can convince old Sakuruta this herd's for his people, he'll turn back, I think. We could catch up with you. Could ride guard on you to Round Mountain." He glanced at the low sun. "Ain't it time you made camp?"

"Not on your life!" Mike said. "I don't like this piece of country. Hollinger claims it's all his range. Good as said we're in trespass and he had the right to cut the herd for strays."

"He's a liar!"

"He's that and a lot more, but he can call on any number of tough nuts to back his play. My crew's no good. Cullen thought he was hiring fighting hands. What he got was trash. Look 'em over when you ride down the herd. Might see some faces you know!"

"Bad as that?"

"Worse. I don't trust 'em not to sell out to Hollinger. And," Mike added, "I've got a woman along. A girl, Cullen's nice. From Colorado. She owns the herd now."

"Man!" Meserve muttered, and whistled softly. "You're right to push on long's you can. It's an early moon, so you can travel late. I'd push on till—well, you know what you're doing." He lifted his reins to ride on south. "Your herd's got to reach Round Mountain! An awful lot depends on it, Gould!"

And that statement, Mike mused, watching him go, was fairly typical of a lawman.

"What in hell does he think I've been trying to do?"

Sleazy sheets of clouds scudding across the night sky hid all but a few stars. In the misty moonlight the slowly moving herd resembled a ghostly army of shambling monsters, horns and eyes shining, the bawling a never-ending grumble.

Joyce, riding up forward to Mike, asked, "Are you going to try crossing the creeks this late?" Her tone, made unnaturally crisp by their strained relationship, verged on demand.

Phin Starr then came up and repeated much the same question. Several creeks cut the trail ahead, Tanker Todd had reported.

Mike, more worried than he cared to admit, frowned up at the sky. Trailing by clear moonlight had been difficult

enough, the herd troublesome, the crew sullen. In this uncertain light its hazards increased hourly. He wouldn't have
attempted it, except that he weighed it as a lesser risk than
making camp on Hollinger's stamping grounds.

He answered curtly, "We cross any creek tonight that's
crossable. We keep going as long as we can."

Starr nodded and dropped back.

Joyce said, "You're taking chances, aren't you?"

"I am," he agreed. "Got to." A sudden wrath rose in him,
born of worry, strain, weariness, lack of sleep. "Taking
chances with your herd, you mean!" He turned and looked
at her, his eyes burning in their dark, hollow circles. "Soon's
I get this herd in the clear, it's all yours! You can keep my
pay!"

"Let's not be—"

"I'm finding out there are some things I won't do for
money!" he interrupted her roughly. "One of 'em is to work
for a woman—to go on working for a woman who mistrusts
my judgment!"

'But I don't really—"

"I wish I could quit right now! You and I don't get along,
Miss Cullen!"

She trembled, and put a hand up to her throat. "We don't
seem to, do we? I'm sorry," she whispered, turning her face
from him. "I—I'll go back to the wagon."

He was immediately regretful, but could find nothing to
say that would heal the bruise of his words, and he watched
her ride toward the rear where her wagon now followed
the herd. His outburst, he realized, was directed at her from
pent-up feelings and frustrations, of which she was the cause.

She looked small and forlorn, fading off into the near
darkness. Mike swung around and started after her, still
having no idea of what to say, hoping to think of something. Starr delayed him with questions concerning the next
creek ahead.

"It's shallow," Mike told him impatiently, moving on.

Next, old Tanker Todd reined alongside, peering at him.
"Keep your eyes open, Gould!" he mumbled. "I prospect
trouble!"

"What kind?"

Tanker Todd shook his head and reined off. His mumble
floated back: "Watch out for that gal!"

Frowning, Mike touched up his horse and rode on down
the herd, trying to locate Joyce. Tanker Todd's warning had

sounded genuine, but he wasn't a very reliable source of information. No telling what notion might enter the head of a burned-out old boozer. Still, he'd know of it if the crew was plotting mischief. He was one of them.

A swaying, flickering glow brightened rapidly at the tail end of the herd. It burst, a sheet of flame, a traveling bonfire rushing up behind the loose horses of the remuda. The panicked horses, a scramble of black silhouettes, plunged up through the drag, pursued by the fire. Laggard steers jumped, raced with the horses in a bellowing, squealing tumult.

It all happened in a moment. One crushing thought lodged in Mike's mind—*It's come!*—before a vast ripple of terror swept through the whole length of the herd.

He slung his horse aside and it tried to bolt with him. The trail was a deafening chute of hurtling cattle. He saw the flash of a gun. A pair of riders streaked by. Two of the crew. They passed without seeing him, or without recognizing him in the dust-filled darkness. He got the impression that they were laughing.

I have lived through this before! he thought dully. It was like the repetition of a nightmare. He held his shivering horse at halt, looking at chaos, until the last of the herd roared by and vanished. Down the trail an overturned wagon burned. The big Cullen wagon, team gone, a few bits of leather harness curling in the heat of the fire. *It has happened again!*

He went searching for Joyce, calling her name, and found her when she called back to him. She stood leaning against her trembling horse, clinging to its reins and saddle, her head drooping. He dismounted and put his arm around her to steady her, wondering in despair how badly she was injured, cursing himself for letting her turn back.

"You're hurt! Where?"

She raised a blood-smeared face to him. "My forehead—I'll be all right. My horse bolted with me and smashed into a thicket. Two of the men were chasing me."

He thought of the two laughing riders. "Same ones who set fire to your wagon?"

"I think so. It was burning before I got to it." She held her head, and made motions at brushing back her disheveled hair. Her hat was gone. "They must have thrown coal oil over it. No driver. The team ran—"

"I know," he said heavily.

"Is everything gone?"

"Everything but us! And we're in poor shape!" He helped her up onto her horse, tested the cinch, examined the animal's legs. Straightening up, he said in weary self-disgust, "I'm the big hombre who took on to get your herd through to Round Mountain. Two herds I've lost, yours and mine. Two! Now you're as broke as I am. Wiped out—this close to delivery! I oughta crawl the rest o' my life!"

"Don't blame yourself, Mike."

"I do!"

"If there's any blame, it's on my uncle, God rest him. He hired Starr and the others, instead of picking experienced and dependable cowpunchers as he should have done."

Mike shook his head. "It's time I was honest with you. Sure, your uncle picked the wrong crew, but I made myself trail boss. When I met up with your outfit I was strictly on the make. I purposely riled your uncle and led Starr into taking a swing at me. Why? To make it easy for me to claim mavericker's pay for the cows I'd found, that's why!"

She nodded slowly. "I think I can understand that. Besides, you had a grudge against my uncle for outbidding you on cattle and supplies at Lost Creek."

"I was sour at him, yes, but it was the money—"

"And probably sour at me, too, for hitting you with my buggy whip!"

"I didn't know at the time you were traveling along with the outfit. Frankly, I doubted you were his niece. Anyhow, I took it out on Starr, and after I got through with him the outfit needed a new boss. I took the job on. I fell down on it! Licked to a finish, on the last lap!"

She leaned down to him from her saddle. "Licked?" she said fiercely into his face. "I didn't think Mike Gould would ever admit to that! Licked by a worthless trail crew? Well, I'm not! Not yet!"

He looked back into her face, and drew a breath. Her eyes were blazing. He asked her, "What d'you figure you can do?"

"They must have some idea of holding the herd together and driving it somewhere to sell. I'm going to find out!"

"That's what I was doing when I found your missing cows," he told her wryly. "I was looking for my herd. Didn't get to finish the search. What'll you do if you find out where your herd's gone?"

"I don't know, but it will be a start! Anything is better than giving up!"

He sighed, tired out and no longer sure of himself. "How many busted Texans have I heard say that!"

She straightened up, shook her hair back, drew the reins purposefully between her fingers. Not looking at him, she remarked, "I've heard it said that Mexico fancies it could whip the United States, if only Texas would keep still. Is that just a brag made by Texans?"

"Most likely. Sounds like it." He paused, and asked her quietly, "Are the hungry Pawnees at Round Mountain on your mind? Are you thinking what can happen if they don't get beef? Or is it the money?"

"The money doesn't seem so important to me now," she answered.

He nodded. "Nor to me, I find. We appear to be getting to understand each other better. Or maybe we've both changed some, now we're both down to hardpan. Short time back, you jumped on me for taking chances with your herd. Now I've lost the whole kit and caboodle, you don't lay the blame of it on me."

"No man could do more than you've done, Mike."

"Thank you, Joyce," he said. "I wasn't actually about to give up. Just tired." He legged onto his horse. "Okay, let's go."

She nudged her horse into step with his. "Please forget what I said about bragging Texans."

He fetched up a grin for her. "When Texans quit bragging, that'll be the day Colorado falls off Pike's Peak!"

CHAPTER ELEVEN

The torn-up trail wore a strange appearance, deserted and silent after the thunderous tumult of the stampede. A steer's trampled corpse bulked shapeless on the ground. Rain pattered, ceased; the clouds shredded and the moon broke through.

Mike said to Joyce, "The herd stayed bunched this far, I guess. Kept to the trail. Habit. The creeks will have scattered 'em, though."

They reached the first creek. The banks were steep, darkly overhung with brush and tree-growth, but users of the trail in past years had cut down the banks here at the shallow fording. Mike studied the ground, frowning at deeply scarred and churned earth.

"Wait here," he told Joyce, and crossed over to the north bank. The water rose to his stirrups, receded; he rode onto dry ground that bore no fresh tracks, not one wet mark. Not a cow in the herd had crossed the creek, nor horse nor man. That was a curious circumstance. A creek could split up stampeding cattle and horses, but some of them would splash on over unless headed off by other means, other obstacles.

Returning to the south bank, his searching attention fastened onto pale objects lying in the mud. He had missed noticing them when crossing the creek, they being upstream behind him. He dismounted to examine them. They were large squares of canvas tacked to pole frames, fringed with streamers of white cotton. He picked up one of them. His horse shied from it.

Joyce rode along the lower bank and joined him, catching the reins of his nervous horse. "What's that?" she asked.

"Stampeders' equipment!" he explained to her bleakly, throwing the thing down, ramming the heel of his boot through the canvas. "They're up to every trick!"

"But the herd was already stampeded before it got here!"

"Yeah! They burned your wagon to start it off. They had men posted here, ready to turn the herd off from scattering out or crossing the creek. Did it with these, flapping 'em as the cows showed up. They turned the herd here, east along the creek. Starr and the crew, and others in on it—it was all worked out. They only missed catching you. Don't think they won't be out to finish the score! I'm not saying it to rattle you, but—"

"And you?"

"Well, yes. They figured I'd be up front, set for tromping or a bullet. So happened I turned back looking for you."

"I'm glad you did," she said. In the next instant she exclaimed, "What was that?"

The sound, a slow scrape and jingle of a spurred boot, whirled Mike around, his gun out. He rapped, "Who's there?"

"Me!" the hoarse voice of Tanker Todd answered him. "Don't waste a shell. I'm shot. Can't move."

They discovered the old boozer under the bank, lying face down in loose dirt. Mike eased him over onto his back. "How'd you get shot?" he asked.

"Damn simple! Phin Starr did it. Gunned me down an' kicked me off the bank." Tanker Todd breathed noisily. "He saw me talk to you, maybe heard what I said. I knew the bust was coming up. Hell, that was all right, only I'm too old to 'preciate what was in store for the young missy, there. Taking a Texas herd is one thing, but—"

"You were all in on that, eh? Right from the first, before Hollinger showed up?"

"Long before! When we hired out to Cullen, before he started for Texas to buy cattle, it was on orders from Hollinger. Cullen never had a chance. Starr had orders what to do. Let Cullen sink his money in cattle, then bust him. Make things go wrong, and delay the herd." He grinned weakly. "We weren't ever lost, Gould. We knew where to take that herd and when we'd be expected. Orders! If you knew who Hollinger is—"

"I've been told he's kingpin of the Jayhawkers," Mike said.

"You were told right!"

"I wouldn't have taken you for a Jayhawker."

"Did you think we all run to the same pattern?" Todd asked dryly. "We got all kinds, from Hollinger himself down to a busted old tinhorn like me. I don't stand high." He paused to take breath. "You put a crimp in our timing. Hollinger wasn't ready. He's a busy man. He had to change the plan some. Then those Pawnees cropped up, and he had to make another change. It's worked out for him, but he'll give Starr hell for letting you two get away!"

Mike nodded. "Did Starr kill Cullen, back there on the Cimarron?"

"You figure it. I know Cullen wasn't to get home alive. Starr got in touch with Hollinger. Sent a report. Lew Keeley and his men came out to settle you and take over the herd, us helping Hollinger gave it his personal attention. You're a tough duck, but it's lucky for you the Pawnees came along."

Mike squatted thinking of Harley Cullen. That man of good intentions and bad judgment never stood a chance, as Todd said. He had taken on a band of Jayhawkers, in the belief that he was hiring a fighting crew to protect his herd. Wolves to guard a flock of sheep. Hollinger had ordered his death, and arranged for the herd to be delivered right at his own back door at his convenience, chillingly businesslike.

Tanker Todd muttered, cursing Starr for gunning him down without warning. Presently he said, "Hey, am I dying?" A short silence, and he answered himself, "Guess I am."

Mike couldn't think of anything to say. After a few moments he drew Joyce aside. "I'm setting out to track the herd now," he told her. "Won't be hard. They ran east. Tired as they are, they won't go far. I could still hear their rumble, till the breeze died."

"We're setting out," she corrected him.

"You stay back! No knowing what I'll run into. I don't want to have to worry about you if anything pops."

"You wouldn't worry about leaving me behind? How safe is it for me here?"

He scrubbed his bristled jaw with the palm of his hand. "Could hide you—"

"For how long? You might not get back!"

"Maybe you could make it on up to Hopewell."

"Maybe!" Her eyes suddenly blazed. "We're both going together! You can't stop me!"

He gazed at her, for the moment forgetful of catastrophe.

"One minute you're a young lady, the next you're a wildcat!"

"Forget the young lady! I'm going with you to find the herd. I can ride, and if I have to I can shoot! Forget I'm a girl, will you? For now?"

He went on gazing at her. "How can I?" He drew her up close to him and kissed her on the mouth, hard. Feeling her ready response, the blood rushed to his head. Releasing her at last, he said huskily, "Should I say I'm sorry? I'm not."

"No." She raised fingertips to her lips, her face, made tender by his bristly pressure.

"I'm only sorry that we—that the time and place—"

"Yes." Her face flamed scarlet. "I understand."

He went back to Tanker Todd. The man was dead. Mike took the gun and belt from the body, and rejoined Joyce. "Strap this gun on. We'll scout down the creek. Eyes and ears open, mind! The moon's still high. If we're spotted, you cross the creek any place you can and cut north. We might have to cross before then. Depends on what we find."

Hoofbeats pattered on the trail, coming up from the south. Mike and Joyce halted, tensely listening, watching. Three horsemen rode up to the creek bank and reined in, bending down to examine the cattle tracks as Mike had done. Mike recognized the knotty little figure of Thad Meserve, the U. S. marshal. The two with him were Pawnee men.

Mike called softly, "Meserve!" He rode forward.

The marshal holstered his fast-drawn gun. "What's wrong, Gould? We passed a burned-out wagon, couple of dead steers —" Joyce's horse whickered in the shadows, and his gun instantly reappeared. "Who's that?"

"Harley Cullen's niece," Mike told him. "Joyce Cullen." He paused, hating to give the bad news. "Come on out, Joyce, this is Mr. Meserve, the United States marshal from Round Mountain."

Too preoccupied to do more than touch his hat briefly to her, Meserve asked Mike, "Where's the herd?"

"Lost it!"

He stared aghast at Mike. His face actually paled, and in that minute he looked old and shrunken. He said, his voice low and flat, "I talked with Sakuruta. He told me he came down to see for himself if Cullen was really bringing a beef herd to his people. He and his band have been scouring the country, searching the trails as far west as the Chisholm. I gathered it's his final try at keeping the peace. He can't keep the peace if he has to tell his people they're cheated again! They'll rise!"

"Cullen didn't cheat them!" Mike said.

"How do I tell that to Sakuruta? He doubted me when I told him it was Cullen's herd you were bringing up. He knows Cullen, and didn't see him with the herd."

"He could see we were on the trail to Round Mountain, couldn't he?"

Meserve gestured wearily. "It's Baxter Springs this trail goes to. I took for granted you knew it. Thought you aimed to swing west after you got clear of Hollinger. Sakuruta, not seeing any sign it was Cullen's herd, thought you were a Texas outfit headed for the Baxter Springs market. How about your crew?"

"Jayhawkers, working for Hollinger," Mike answered. "It was all set up. They knew this trail. I didn't. Nor Cullen. They knew when to stampede the herd."

"Two herds you've lost in one trip! That's something of a record, ain't it?"

"Nothing I'm proud of!"

"You shouldn't be!"

Joyce spoke up. "Mr. Meserve, it's no fault of his! That herd was mine, but I'm not blaming him for the loss of it. With a treacherous crew—"

"Miss Cullen!" Meserve snapped. "The blame of it's nothing to me. It's the consequences I'm facing! Sakuruta let me bring two of his warriors, for me to prove to 'em that Gould was taking the herd to Round Mountain. That's the best he'd do. He suspected I was stringing him along. Now they'll go back to—"

He broke off, looking sharply around. "Where are they?" The two silent and stony-faced Pawnees had vanished. A flutter of pony hoofs faded down the trail. "They've gone back," he said, "to tell Sakuruta I'm a liar!"

"Could we go with you and convince him you told the truth?" Joyce asked.

"Only the herd would convince him," he replied harshly. "It's too late for words! They've had their fill of words, promises, explanations. They've lost faith in white men. Even in me, and I'm only half white. They see me as a government man. That cooks me!"

Mike had a suggestion. "Could we talk them into helping us get the herd back?"

Meserve stared at him. "Talk Pawnees into fighting white

men? Damn it, that's just what we don't want! Worse, you're proposing we help 'em take the law into their own hands! We'd be posted as renegades, hunted along with them, wanted dead or alive!"

"But Hollinger and his bunch of—"

"No court's found 'em guilty, has it? Even so, any Indian kills a white man, he's finished. He might's well take the warpath and go on killing while he lasts. Which is about what my Pawnees would do!" He shook his head emphatically. "I hate it, but the only thing left to me now is ask for troops."

"That'll take time," Mike observed.

"Don't I know it! Nearest cavalry I know of is a patrol camped somewhere along the Fort Smith road. Their lieutenant most likely will want orders from his post commander, before he'll trail with me after Sakuruta. The post commander might spend a day or two readying his full force to march out to battle," Meserve said glumly, "or he'll send for orders from division headquarters. And if *they* refer it back to Washington—"

"Then maybe you'd get your troops next spring."

"No, they'd be rushed in long before that. Emergency. A Pawnee uprising, Sakuruta at the head. Full-scale campaign to whip the bloodthirsty savages for treacherously turning on their kindly white brothers for no reason at all!" Meserve's tone dripped bitter sarcasm. "Newspapers back East headlining stories of massacre and torture, written by reporters in St. Louis saloons! Politicians nobly speechifying about the army's duty! Can't trust any Indians! The better you treat 'em, the worse they are! Pawnees? Why, those Pawnee varmints were coddled, fed like nabobs, given a piece of their own land to live on—and now look what they do!"

He reined his horse to the creek. "When you get up to Hopewell, tell the folks there they better be ready to move out!" he called back, and splashed on over, hitting his horse to a run as he reached the north bank.

"We're going to track the herd first, aren't we?" Joyce asked Mike. He hesitated, having a second thought about it, and she insisted, "We can find out where the herd is gone to. We can report it at Round Mountain. The Indian Agent would do all he could to find us help, wouldn't he?"

"I guess so. Of course, by then the herd could be anywhere." He shrugged. "Still, we might get lucky."

CHAPTER TWELVE

The moon was half down when they sat peering out over a valley that, narrow at its west mouth where the creek found exit, appeared to widen out eastward to a flat horizon. It looked peacefully isolated. The creek wound around small islands of trees and low hillocks. Cattle thickly dotted the grass as far as the eye could see to the east. Distantly off to the right, on higher ground, a speck of light indicated the ranch house.

"Good cow country," Mike commented. The tracks of the herd had led directly along the creek to it. "Good cow-thief country! This is one big holding ground. See how it funnels? They can run cattle in at this end, and let 'em turn loose. The cows will paw around some, like they do on any strange range whether they've been stampeded or not, but after a while they settle down to grazing. They don't need any riders to hold 'em in, except off there in the east—and maybe not there if they've strung a fence. At the time that suits Hollinger, his riders can open the fence, if there's one, shove what cattle they want on out the big end and up to his ranch on the Kansas line."

"What about their brands?" Joyce asked.

"Hollinger's worked out a trick to get around that. It saves him from having to work the brands over, and gives him a steady year-round market for the beef." Sensing her wonderment at his knowing, he said, "It was told to me by a man named McChristal. Was a friend of mine once. Gone bad," he added tersely. "So many do, when they lean on a gun too long."

"You didn't."

92

"It was touch and go. I tossed for it, my last half-dollar, and went back to Texas for a fresh start." The memory brought up a thought of Juan Bujac, fast pistolero, one-time hidalgo. Juan had reached the edge, probably gone beyond it, before joining the outfit.

He gazed estimatingly at the cattle in the valley. "There's more than your herd, by far. I'll circle round the slopes and take a look at some brands up yonder. Might find some of mine. This time you stay back. You can't do me any good there."

"Why not?"

"In this light, if I'm spotted there's a good chance they'll take me for one of them. They won't be sure. I'll have time to make a break for it. Not you! There's something about a woman in the saddle that's different. She can ride like a man, but most any man can tell in a minute she's a woman! That is," he amended, "if she's a real woman, which it so happens you are!"

"All right," she agreed reluctantly. "I'll wait here for you."

"Take cover, stay quite, and keep watch. I'll be back soon's I can. If you hear me coming in a hurry, don't wait! Cross the creek and make for the trail north. I'll catch up with you."

He rode the north slopes, taking what advantage he could of shadowed folds and scattered stands of trees. Cover became scarcer as the valley spread out. The cattle had bedded down for the night, only a few of them shifted restlessly, haunted by nervousness.

Coming to a dip, he followed it down to the valley bottom. The nearest bunch of cattle lay some fifty yards off. If any lookouts were around, they'd spot him when he broke out into the open. He gambled on there being none, and put his horse forward at a walk. A steer snorted and rose uneasily onto its legs at his approach, disturbing others into doing the same, ready to run.

Crooning quietly, drawing closer, he saw their earmarks, Texas brands, and the road brand of the Cullen herd. He reined off at once and took to the slopes. Farther on the slopes steepened to bad footing in bare shale that the horse's hoofs dug loose in noisy little showers. He dropped down again and rode the bottom, openly, crooning soothingly to the cattle while catching their brands. With the moon low behind him, he guessed nobody could recognize who he was, but he felt as conspicuous as a bull moose in a snowfield.

Texas brands, all familiar to him, from Lost Creek. More and more of the steers he passed bore the road brand of his own herd. Two herds here in this huge holding ground, this reservoir for stolen cattle. His had been driven in days ago, then got pushed up the valley by the arrival of the Cullen herd. And probably there were some leavings from other stolen herds farther on.

Startlingly, a voice hailed, "Early, ain't you?"

Mike suppressed an immediate instinct to draw his gun. He held his horse to its walk. His eyes darted to three giant oaks, the only cover near, and barely made out the black bulk of of a horseman in the deep shadow under them. He grunted a response, angling over toward the oaks, forcing on himself the lounging casualness of a relief rider.

"What's that you was singing to the critters?" the lookout asked, touching his horse forward. "New one to me."

Mike grunted again, dismounting. He bent, running a hand over his horse's foreleg, keeping his face shielded. The man came alongside, peering down at him. "Who're you? Don't think I've—"

Flattened by distance, a single shot cracked. The man raised his head to stare toward the western end of the valley. "Now what's that mean?"

He began a yell, toppling from his horse, dragged off by his belt. Mike clubbed him with the barrel of his gun and let him fall. The man's riderless horse plunged, raked by the dragged spurs. It bolted toward the cattle, veered off, and went pounding down the valley. Mike jumped on his horse and took after it, abandoning caution. The noise of the runaway made caution useless, but it was the sound of the shot that sent him racing back. A pistol shot. Joyce, perhaps, had fired it to warn him. Or she was in trouble.

He lashed his horse, straining to get out of the valley before the alarm bottled him in, the shot preying heavily on his mind. The slopes drew together, almost meeting at the creek. The runaway ahead dashed on through, vanishing from sight. Riding into the dark gap, he called out, "Joyce!"

No answer. He had told her not to wait if she heard him coming back in a hurry. And that shot . . .

"Pull up, Texan!" a man rapped .

He whipped out his gun and ducked low, glaring about him, his instant impulse to shoot and make a run for it.

Without further warning a shot roared, so close that its flash made murkily visible to him the man behind it. His horse sank head down under him, rolling over as he kicked free of the stirrups.

"Jump him—quick!"

He didn't know how many men piled onto him, crushing him down, gripping his arms and legs, hammering and kicking at him. The butt of a gun rose above his face. They had such fast hold of him, he couldn't even roll his head to dodge the downward stroke.

Hollinger said, "You could be in far worse shape, and still stand trial!"

Mike finished the glass of whiskey that had been set before hime. "Jayhawker trial? I saw the result of one! My segundo, Juan Bujac. Flogged to death."

"So I understand. It should give you some idea of what's coming!"

Mike wiped his face. He had come to his senses soaking wet from a pitcher of water poured over him, slumped in a chair, his head and arms sprawled on a table. The first sight that met his eyes was Joyce, seated in a corner of the room. Hollinger paced the floor as he talked, the bare floorboards creaking under his weight. Lew Keeley and his squad stood looking on. Mike guessed they had brought him to the main room of the ranch house. Its walls, like the floor, were of bare planks. A makeshift headquarters, built for plain utility. The beginnings of daylight glimmered on windows, but two lamps burned.

"If it's all settled," he said, "why hold a trial?"

Hollinger turned in his pacing, looked at him, paced on. "Because I'm the law here! Because it's my command that any miscreant captured alive must stand trial. Because it impresses discipline on my Jayhawkers. Steadies them. Holds them in line. Without law, they'd become like animals, unruly, irresponsible."

"They're worse than animals now!" Mike remembered Juan Bujac's expression for them, and spoke it. *"Animaluchos!* You're using scum to ruin the country!"

Hollinger continued slowly pacing the floor, hands clasped behind his back. He shook his head. "You're wrong. This is a big country, all this. It's meant for big men. Strong men of vision and ambition. Not lazy savages and grubbing settlers! They're the ones who are ruining it. Run them out, I say! Exterminate all such vermin! You Texans ran your Indian tribes out years ago."

"Before my time," Mike said. "That any reason you should make war on Texas trail drivers? Steal their herds?"

"I need the Jayhawkers, and they need to be paid. I'll use any method to restore this country to cattlemen and cattle!" Stopping, Hollinger leveled a finger at Mike. "The end justifies the means!" Then, as if suspecting that he had allowed himself to be placed on the defensive, he barked, "You're a renegade cattleman!"

"How's that?"

"You tried to take a damned settler's herd up to feed mangy Indians! In my book that's worse than killing Witter!"

Mike tightened inside. "So you know about that?"

"We know!" Hollinger said grimly. "You'll stand trial!"

"When?"

"Today. We don't waste time."

"How about"—Mike looked at Joyce—"Miss Cullen? You can't charge her with anything."

"She'll be a witness for the prosecution!"

Lew Keeley spoke up. "Begging your pardon, Mr. Hollinger," he said respectfully, "but I got a charge against her! She nearly put a bullet through me, when we caught her down in the gap!" He moved toward Joyce, rubbing his hands together.

Hollinger nodded. "I'll make a note of that. Put her in the south room and see she gets breakfast. Keep your hands off her. That goes for everybody. Lock Gould in the grain shed. I'll hold court this afternoon."

They staged the trial in the same bleak room, doors and windows wide open to accommodate the Jayhawker mob pressing outside. From the first it was a travesty, yet conducted with all the stern seriousness of an inquisition.

Hollinger presided as judge and prosecutor, both. No jury. No counsel for the defense. Proceedings followed a stark pattern of parading witnesses who testified against the prisoner, solemnly swearing his life away. No cross-examination allowed. Nor was any formal charge lodged against him. Accusations multiplied, were accepted as damning evidence.

A hairy man averred that his Jayhawker band had a score to settle. Down near the South Fork, attending to business, they'd got shot up by Mike and his Mexican segundo. Four killed, one their leader. "We got the Mexican!" He glared at Mike. "Him next! Let's have him!"

A rumble went through the listening Jayhawker mob outside. Hollinger knuckled the table. "Order! This is a trial, and by its due process I'll reach a verdict!" His sketchy smattering of courtroom terms would have sounded ludicrous, except that he spoke with such ponderous gravity, apparently unaware of his own irony. "Justice will be served the prisoner!" he proclaimed.

Mike marveled at his control over the Jayhawkers. They were wild men, outlaws, and yet Hollinger had drilled into them a kind of self-righteous conceit that approached his own sweeping egotism. It gave them a sense of superiority, a spirit of privilege that justified their most appalling deeds. When thwarted in their plundering, beaten off, they became the injured ones, aggrieved, demanding vengeance.

Joyce sprang to her feet. "Justice? This isn't a trial!" She stepped forward, raising a shaking finger at Hollinger. "It's a mockery! You're—"

"Quiet!" he barked.

"I'll not be quiet! This is not a courtroom, and you're not a judge!" Her voice rose higher, while the mob muttered again, crowding the doors and windows. "You're holding a mock trial to condemn Milk Gould for defending himself from your cutthroats and thieves! Law? You don't know the meaning of it!"

Hollinger half rose from his chair. "As a prejudiced witness, hostile to this court, I rule that you—"

"Somebody must speak up for him against their lies and your hypocrisy!"

He pounded the table before him. In the dark red of his face, his protruding eyes were pale glass marbles. "I'll hold you in contempt!"

"I already hold you in contempt!" she flashed, and Mike caught his breath. She had gone too far. In her hot indignation she had cast an insult that was unforgivable to a man of Hollinger's nature. An insult before a crowd of his men. The aptness of it stirred up a snuffling chuckle here and there, quickly suppressed.

The color receded from Hollinger's face. His big hands spread flat on the table. "Young woman, you'll regret that!" he promised softly, and sank back into his chair. "Next witness!"

A man came on who spoke of the killing of Witter. "We tracked McChristal, found him drunk in a brush camp. Said he took Gould to the shack. Witter was there. Gould killed him and got away. McChristal swore to it."

Joyce was up on her feet again. "That's not evidence! It's only hearsay, passed from one man to another!"

Hollinger reached up to a quirt that hung on the wall. He drew it through his fingers, staring at her. Mike tensed to jump at him. The next instant the quirt struck him in the face. "You'll get that any time she talks out of turn!" Hollinger said. "Better tell her to keep quiet!"

Joyce sat down, white-faced, gazing at Mike and biting her lip. Hollinger asked the man, "Where's McChristal now?"

"We shot him!" was the answer. "It was his doing, taking Gould to the shack. He knew it. He was hiding out, figuring on a long night's ride. The booze slowed him."

Hollinger nodded, hanging up the quirt. "This court," he pronounced, "has heard all the evidence!" His heavy tone issued it with the finality of a royal proclamation. "This court, constituted and empowered by law to serve justice, has, in its dignity"—he slid a baleful look at Joyce—"given impartial hearing to the facts of the case." His pause was deliberate, for effect. The outside mob stilled, captured by his psuedo-learned phrases, his blatant pompousness that passed for imperious authority. "This court has reached the verdict!"

He opened a ledger on the table, dipped a pen in a brass inkwell, went through the motions of inscribing for the record.

"I find the prisoner guilty of murder!"

The mob broke out an uproar, cheering the verdict and clamoring for the sentence of execution. By whip. By fire. Somebody proposed flaying the condemned prisoner, skinning him alive, loudly asserting that he knew how, having once lived with a Blackfoot tribe away off up in Idaho.

"You filthy hypocrite!" Joyce screamed at Hollinger. "You're worse than your killers!" She started running to Mike.

Lew Keeley caught her wrist and pulled her around to him. "I reckon you're mine!" he said.

Phin Starr burst into the room, shouting, "No, she ain't! Goddamit, she's mine! My crew'll tell you, right from the first I've—"

"I caught her!"

"It was me brung her up here! I've earned her!"

A hand on the hilt of his sheathed knife, the hairy Jayhawker from the South Fork interposed, "If she's for free, I'm staking my claim!"

Hollinger banged the table for silence, and got it. "Lay off, before you tear her apart among you!" he commanded. "Hold onto the prisoner! This court is still in session."

He closed the ledger, brushed back his thick yellow hair, and reverted to his stilted, cumbersome style of speech, evidently fond of it.

"The court takes cognizance of the young woman's connection with the case in hand, of her disrespect to me, and her impertinent attempts to discredit reputable witnesses!" he said, rolling out the phrases. The mob listened attentively. "It is aware that she's an object of interest to many of you. It will be merciful, and make arrangements for her care."

Keeley and Starr both made to speak. Hollinger cut them off. "Quiet—I'm passing sentence! For Gould, the death penalty!"

He waited for a roar of approval to subside, and said to Mike, "You're a fighting man, so I'll let you have your fill of fighting. I sentence you to meet all comers, barehanded! All those who want to will draw numbers for their turn at you. You'll fight them, one after another, until you're dead!"

"But the girl!" Keeley persisted. "How about the girl?"

Hollinger steepled his fingertips. "Yes. For her, this court tempers justice with mercy, imposing no punishment for her offenses," he said benignly, while the balls of his eyes bulged, fixed on her. "However, she must be restrained from, er, from committing more mischief! The fights with Gould will settle that problem."

He stood up, holding them all hushed, waiting for his next words. Something like icy humor underlay the stare he aimed at Mike, then back at Joyce.

"I order that she be turned over into the custody of the man who kills Gould! The man will be personally responsible for—"

Half a dozen alert men swarmed on Mike as he lunged at Hollinger, who stood unmoved.

CHAPTER THIRTEEN

They opened the bouts in the yard, the Jayhawker mob forming a ring, after time spent in drawing numbered slips from a hat, and much discussion over the right to trade them back and forth. A general argument broke out, some favoring a time limit to give as many men as possible the chance of a crack at Mike.

The final vote set the limit at fifteen minutes to a fight, no breaks, nothing barred. Down a man by any means at all, then use the boots, gouge him, strangle him. The dire prospect weeded out a few prudent ones and thinned the waiting list.

Stripped to the waist, Mike faced the first contender, one of the Keeley squad. Hollinger, gold watch in hand, called, "Go to it!"

The man was young, with hot and reckless eyes. He rushed in slugging, overeager to win at the first onslaught and throwing all he had into it. Mike straight-armed him off, and stepped back to give him space for another fist-swinging rush, letting him spend his steam. He met it with a reaching left, and again moved clear.

Furious, the young man lowered his head and charged. Mike dodged, taking a swipe at him as he went by, and passing over to the other side of the ring. The onlookers presently grew restive, watching his tactics. They wanted to see blood.

"Call this a fight?" somebody complained. "Gould's stalling!"

"Saving his strength!" Keeley drawled. "Maybe he can stretch it out till it's my turn at him!"

"The youngun ain't hardly hit him yet!"

Mike ducked a high roundhouse blow, but caught one in his middle. He lashed out twice. He had meant to make the fight last its full fifteen minutes, saving himself for the fights to come, although knowing that his end was inevitable. No man could survive an unbroken chain of fresh opponents. One of them would down him, finish him off. All he could do was hold out as long as possible, clinging to a tiny shred of hope that something might yet come up that he could work into a chance for life. He owed it to Joyce. Her downfall was tied directly to his, by Hollinger's malevolent mockery of justice. The man who conquered him won Joyce as the prize, it amounted to that, and Hollinger had provided it as an incitement, knowing that the most depraved of his men would be the most eager contenders.

Retaliating for the body blow, Mike struck too hard. The young man crumpled, agony twisting his face, the beserk rage knocked out of him. On the ground, he cast a shrinking look at Mike's boots, and crawled out of the ring into the legs of the jeering mob.

"Number two!" Hollinger called, and number two stepped in, grinning, spitting on his hands, plainly intending to rely on wrestling rather than fist-fighting.

He was a burly Jayhawker, stripped to the waist like Mike, a thick pelt of black hair covering his chest and arms. On his feet he wore moccasins, and he had bound his hair into a knot, Indian fashion. "Gonna tear ye to leetle bits!" he vowed, shambling forward, knees bent and arms bowed.

Mike changed his tactics. Taking the offensive, he leaped in and hit him low in the stomach, a hard-driving left, and bringing his right foot forward he rammed his heel down on a moccasin. The surprised Jayhawker let out a bellowing gasp and grabbed at him. Mike uppercut him alongside the jaw, jabbed him in the eye, and broke clear to look him over. His aim was to take the edge off the man right away, disable him, slow him up before he got warmed. Those powerful arms could crush ribs in, once they gripped hold. The fingernails had raked him like talons.

One eye streaming, the Jayhawker limped after him. He worked his hurt jaw, growling. He had the middle of the ring, and holding his big arms spread forward he tried to trap Mike into close quarters. Mike ducked off. With designs on the other eye, he spun around and struck fast.

He missed. His fist landed square on the low forehead,

and the numbing shock of it ran up his arm. Thick fingers snapped around his wrist. The Jayhawker was as swift and agile as an ape. All he needed was one hold to build on, and now he had it.

"Gotcha!"

Mike threw himself backward, tugging him onto his crushed foot, but couldn't free his numbed left arm. He foresaw its bones getting broken, the beginning of the end, this white savage monstrously claiming Joyce. He kicked him in the groin.

Nobody raised a word of objection. He could expect the same brutal punishment, and worse, from any man coming against him. All-out fighting, nothing barred. Some of the onlookers, waiting their turn at him and not wanting him finished ahead of them, cheered ironically.

Doubling over, hissing through his teeth, the Jayhawker slipped his grip on Mike's wrist. Mike jabbed him in the other eye. He walked around him, rubbing feeling back into his arm. It had to be ready for the next bout. This one was done. He was expected to finish off the stumbling Jayhawker, but he held off, gaining time. Shadows were long, the sun sinking. If he was still on his feet when darkness fell, Hollinger would have to call it off for the night.

"Time!" Hollinger announced presently.

"We haven't gone the fifteen minutes yet!" Mike said.

Hollinger ignored his protest. "Pull that man out, and get number three in there!" he ordered.

At first glance number three didn't look like much of a fighter. He hadn't the physical equipment. His arms were short, his legs stumpy, attached to a long body. He had practically no neck, and his head was round and bald. Lacking the reach for able fist-fighting, and not having the build of a wrestler, still he stamped into the ring with such businesslike confidence that Mike guessed he must have a trick or two that made him a lot more formidable than he looked.

He stuck his fists up shoulder high, elbows bent, wide open for a body punch. The mob silenced, watching him, some of the men nudging one another. Mike threw a poke at him for experiment, to get him to show what he had. He dodged it nimbly, and came on. As he closed in, the rays of the sinking sun picked out old scars and dents in his bald head.

His hands shot out and grasped Miks' arms. Yanking Mike toward him, he lowered his head and drove it at his face.

A butting man. One butt, and a fight was over. The scars and dents had warned Mike at only the last second; too late to do more than raise his forearms, he took the impact on them. Like a battering-ram, the scarred head drove his own forearms smash into his face.

He broke the man's hold and fell back, his nose gushing blood. Staying clear, giving himself time to recover, he took advantage of his longer reach to shoot straight punches. Instead of dodging, the man's method was to block them full-on with the top of his head with the intention of breaking Mike's knuckles. It accounted for some of the scars. His head could take blows like a brick wall.

Mike changed to swinging long uppercuts, and connected. The butting battler stalked him doggedly, trying to close in. When he raised his head he showed a face that was beaten raw. His feet began dragging, and once he stumbled into the enclosing mob. Hands shoved him back.

At last Hollinger called, "Time!" He glanced toward the setting sun. "Number four, and make it fast!"

The fourth man was lean, of Mike's build and height, and he evidently had sized up Mike's tactics. He took the stance of a wrestler, but as soon as Mike came at him he snapped out a punch and became an efficient fist-fighter. He followed through with a fast right that knocked Mike across the ring.

There could be no stalling off this one, no saving of strength and wind. He was a tiger, pressing the fight, setting a fast pace and never letting down. Mike got in a hard left that shook him, but missed with a right, and that brought them into close quarters, jabbing and hooking until they both fell back for breath.

A fist cracked Mike on his jaw like an explosion. He swung wild, steadied himself, landed a belly blow, and tried to dodge clear for a spell. The pace was ruining him. His arms felt heavy, and the spring was out of his legs. A muddlement dulled his ringing head. He needed rest badly, if only for a moment.

The bruiser would have none of that. He was wearing down, his punches lacking some of their former snap, but his legs seemed tireless. He followed Mike, outmaneuvered him, forced him to a standstill. They slugged at each other, toe to toe.

No longer attempting any guard, and meeting none, Mike mechanically traded blow for blow in what had sunk to a punishing contest of endurance. He didn't even feel anger anymore, nothing but a sick and weary will to survive. Darkness dimmed his sight. A narrowing margin of sense told him the blows he was taking were feeble now, not much more than heavily scraping taps.

Then he was hitting at empty air, and looking down he saw the bruiser lying on the ground. He started to turn away, and his knees buckled under him. Spent, gasping, he knelt swaying.

Somebody yelled, "Let me at him—I'm number five!"

It brought a storm of objections from others on the list. Mike Gould, they argued, wasn't on his feet. Too easy for number five, a gift to him, no fight at all.

Hollinger settled it. "This is an execution, not a game!" he sternly reminded them. "But I grant that its conditions demand a fair chance to those taking part in it. It's getting dark, so take Gould back to the grain shed and bring him out in the morning!"

Unable to sleep, Mike stirred restlessly on a pallet of empty grain sacks in the dark. Each movement brought aching torture, but his body was too racked by pains and hurts to lie still in one position for long. Nobody had offered him food or water, and he saw no prospect that anyone would bring him some, late as it was now. They had simply thrown him in, half senseless, his hurts untended, and padlocked the door. Hollinger's orders, he guessed. No charity for the condemned prisoner.

His throat was parched. He climbed to his feet and began a hopeless search for water, for anything drinkable, if only slops left in a bucket. Moving about in the dark, he tripped over a hard and unyielding object. He cursed drearily, lying where he had fallen, striving to locate himself in his surroundings as he had seen them that morning before taken out to stand trial.

The grain shed was the size of a small barn, windowless, with a high gable roof, tightly built to withstand rainstorms. Most of the floor space was taken up by solid piles of sacked grain, leaving a ten-foot passage to the door. Hollinger plainly favored graining his horses well, and no doubt he supplied grain to the Jayhawkers. Like a cavalry commander, he needed to store vast amounts to keep hundreds of horses in condition for hard riding.

What he had tripped over, Mike decided, was a log, canted aslant across the ten-foot passage. Although Hollinger had the foresight to store up tons of grain, he didn't have men who knew or cared enough to stack it properly. A segment of one high pile had threatened to give way like a badly built wall, and they had jammed the log against it to prop it up, rather than go to the trouble of stacking it all over again.

Mike thought of using the log to batter the door open. He had to reject that idea. Take away the log, and he'd have a ton or two of sacked grain collapsing down on him. He felt it gingerly to find out if he had knocked it loose.

"All I need now is to bury myself!" he muttered.

A small sound reached him from the door. A metallic sound. He lay motionless, listening, his senses keyed up, snatching at the faintest hope. It came again, a slight scrape of metal on metal. Someone outside the door was meddling with the padlock, furtively fitting the key, turning it.

The padlock clicked. He listened to further muffled sounds, before the door slowly opened. In the dim rectangle a big shape moved, noiselessly entered, and the door closed. A match scraped, flared. By its light he recognized the hairy face of the Jayhawker from the South Fork. His faint hope died. He watched him take out a stub of candle, light it, set it on the floor, and straighten up. He dipped a look at his waist, another hope rising in him.

The big Jayhawker grinned knowingly. "No, I didn't bring no gun—you'd grab for it! We don't want no noise." He cocked up his left fist. "I got this!" Over his knuckles he wore a heavy brass knuckle-duster.

"Couldn't you wait till tomorrow?" Mike asked him. "And d'you figure you've got to have that damn thing, the shape I'm in?"

He shook his head. "This is to keep you quiet an' peaceable! You know I could kill you with it, nobody the wiser, so don't you get no smart notions!" From inside his coat he produced a flat canteen, army issue, and tossed it over. "Drink!"

Mike unscrewed the stopper and drank water that was liberally laced with whiskey. A package landed beside him.

"Bread an' meat. Eat hearty! An' I brung some liniment. Horse liniment. Stings like hell, you rub it on, but it'll loosen you up for the mornin'."

He wolfed the food down, drank again, and felt better. Finding that he was leaning his back against the log prop, he shifted his seat on the floor. The Jayhawker brandished his knuckle-duster warningly.

"Stay where you're at, an' get busy on the liniment!" He brought the candle closer and set it down. "I'll tell you 'bout the feller who's taking you on first thing in the mornin'. Number five. Watch him! You gotta be lively with that'n!"

Mike applied the liniment, dousing it on himself and rubbing it in, wincing, feeling as if bathing in liquid fire.

The Jayhawker looked on critically. He squatted beside the candle. "Burns, huh? That's part of it, an' the sting. Gotta burn an' sting, or she's no good. I know that feller, number five, right well. He's a kicker. I've seen him kick a standin' man in the face! Does it kinda spinnin' on his other foot. He learned how from a Frenchman, he says."

Mike contemplated going up against a spinning high-kicker. Jump in and crowd him, don't give him room. In-fighting, that was the answer. "Today," he said, "you stood witness against me and howled for my blood! Now you fix me up to beat this number five friend of yours!"

"Yeah. Hollinger'd have my hide, he ever knew I swiped the key, brung you grub, drink, liniment, put you wise on your next fight! I took a chance, Texan!"

"Why?" Mike asked. And then he knew why, from the look on the hairy face.

The Jayhawker cracked a ferocious grin. "After number five, I'm next! I traded for number six—traded everything but my saddle! It'll be worth it! I got fightin' tricks like you never saw, Texan!" He poked Mike's outstretched foot. "Worth it? Hell, I'll profit on the trade! I got a dugout down off South Fork, that all it wants is a woman!"

CHAPTER FOURTEEN

Mike withdrew his foot, then the other, and bringing both knees up he rested his hands on them, staring into the face of the Jayhawker. Like a drowning man reviewing in a flash the whole course of his past, he foresaw the atrocious evils of the future. Tomorrow his defeat and death. Joyce the slave of this foul brute and his South Fork pack of *animaluchos*. Degraded and health-broken. Her death a prayed-for mercy.

Hollinger had surely reckoned on the like of that. To the man daring to cross him, death by beating. Set an example as a standing threat to others. He had extended his hatred of Cullen to Cullen's niece, she having rashly shown her contempt for him. He would go on pursuing his obsession to become the biggest cattle king in the country, a great man of power, crushing all who stood in his way. With success, he could climb to the dignity of a respected state governor.

Watching Mike closely, the Jayhawker poised his big brass-knuckled fist. "Don't jump me! You'll get this!" He picked up the lighted candle, making ready to rise and leave. "Kick me the canteen an' liniment bottle!"

Hands braced on knees, putting all the strength left in his legs and arms, Mike launched himself backward. His bare shoulders collided into the slanted log prop behind him. He felt the butt-end of it dislodge and slide on the floor, and flopping over he scrambled for safety. The sliding log got in his path. He banged against it, knocked it further askew, and floundered on.

The top end of the log fell toward the Jayhawker. He caught it in one powerful hand while he still squatted, his other hand holding the candle. Not hearing it fall, Mike twisted his head for a look.

The Jayhawker glared at him. "What the hell you up to?" he growled, more puzzled than angry. He either hadn't heeded the log, in the weak light of the candle, or didn't realize what it was there for, and Mike's seemingly senseless action confused him.

Ever so slowly, the wall of sacked grain bulged outward in the middle, forced by the weight above. Mike dared not shift his eyes to it. He had time to say, "Thought I saw a snake."

The Jayhawker instinctively lowered his stare to the floor. Above him, the wall broke like a slow and silent explosion, a burst bubble of hundred-pound sacks. The first of them tumbled between him and Mike, blocking the passage and hiding their sight of each other.

Mike heard him start a curse. By the flickering light of the candle he got a glimpse of the weakened stack collapsing at the top and avalanching down. He backed along the passage as far as he could go. The light went out. A muffled voice died in the black darkness, while the soft slithers and thuds continued. Men would have a sweaty job laying up the stack again, and they were due for a surprise when they uncovered what lay buried under it.

The sounds ended. Clambering over the jumbled sacks, Mike felt his way to the door and stopped to listen. He half hoped that the muted noise might have brought somebody to look into it, so that he could jump him for his gun. Nobody came. The grain shed, built near the horse corrals, was over the hill from the house and the bunkhouses.

He eased out, found the padlock hung on the hasp, and locked the door behind him. The Jayhawker had the key, and if there was only one they'd have to break the door open. Cautiously, he prowled up the hill and peered down at the buildings.

Lamps burned in the headquarters house. Here and there a cigarette glowed in the darkness outside the bunkhouses, and a mutter of voices reached him. Four men crossed the yard, were spoken to by another man who emerged from the house. The four moved off, separating. These people kept late hours, perhaps took spells at standing guard the night through, their business being what it was. No chance to approach the house, nor to get hold of a gun here.

Shivering in the cool night air, he picked at the problem

of what to do. He could make it on foot up to Round Mountain, but by the time some good came of that, if any, his escape would be long discovered and Joyce could be anywhere, far and forever out of reach. No, that wasn't the answer. She was down there in a back room of the house, he was here alive, and that covered the last and only chance.

"Got to have a gun!" he breathed. With a gun he could try crawling down behind the house, timing it when the men relaxed watch in the small hours. Break Joyce out, cover her getaway. He didn't want to live with the memory of leaving her behind in Jayhawker hands.

His probing cogitation veered to Tanker Todd. He had taken dead Todd's gun and given it to Joyce, but he hadn't searched the body for other weapons. A man of Todd's kind was apt to pack a hideout pistol somewhere about him, if only a pocket derringer, for insurance. Maybe an armpit gun.

Giving the house a final look, hating to leave, Mike hurriedly set out for salvage. There had to be some kind of gun on Tanker Todd, he told himself. There just had to be. A two-shot derringer wouldn't be much, but anything was better than nothing.

Slogging it on foot, the trek back to the gap seemed long to him, and a lot longer still from there to the trail crossing the creek. At first stiff and sore, his legs limbered up to where he was able to maintain a steady gait, pausing every so often to listen. The fact that the Keeley squad had caught Joyce at the gap indicated that the route was watched and guarded, at least after a stolen herd was run through. On the other hand, the capture of Joyce and himself removed the necessity to guard it.

The moon was gone. Rough walking in the dark was any horseman's idea of the nearest thing to hell, and as a horseman Mike disliked walking in any form. He bared his burning feet and cooled them off in the creek, trying not to think of the long tramp back. Tugging on his worn-out boots, he went along under the creek bank. Tanker Todd's body lay where he had left it, and he fell to searching it, ransacking the pockets, then every likely and unlikely hiding place.

His thorough search turned up no gun, no weapon of any kind except a clasp knife, its single blade gummy and brown from cutting plug tobacco. Tanker Todd had not carried hideout-gun insurance, relying on his six-shooter.

Sunk in a dull rage of despair, Mike sat turning the clasp

knife over and over in his hand. He had felt so sure of his hunch. With every step of the way his belief in it had increased. Here he would find the means to break Joyce out of the Jayhawker stronghold. Had he not felt as positive of it, he wouldn't have stopped to bathe his feet.

A false hunch. Even his hunches had gone sour on him. He raised the knife to hurl it into the creek, thought better of it, and searched for a stone with which to sharpen the blade. It was a kind of weapon, anyhow. If he was going back—and he was—it might come in useful. A last chip sometimes proved lucky. He found a flat stone and set to work putting an edge on the blade, an edge that would cut a throat in a slash.

A hand touched him on his bare shoulder.

He jumped and whirled around. So did Sakuruta jump, but backward, spry as a young buck, wary of the outthrust knife. The old Pawnee chief said in his concise English, "My gun is quicker, Mike Gould!"—running the two names together as one and pronouncing it curiously like "Makegold."

Mike glimpsed the gun in the bony hand, pointed at him. He considered throwing the knife, wanting that gun badly. To do so, he would have to whip back his arm. And the distance was wrong for a spin. It would have to be a slip-throw.

Reading his intention, Sakuruta said, "Look around!"

Mike looked. Cloaked figures stood all about, quiet as rocks. Remembering their reputation as scouts, he could only guess how they had got there without his hearing them. He heaved a sigh, closing the clasp knife, and asked bleakly, "How was the beef?"

"It was good!"

"You want your silver ring back? It's all I've got, and not worth killing me for!"

Sakuruta's sunken black eyes chilled. "I traded the ring for the beef!"

"Yeah. All I've got to show for the whole damn herd! Did your two warriors tell you about it, or didn't they understand what I said to Meserve?"

"Most Pawnees know your tongue. I was taught by a Black Robe—a missionary—long ago. Yes, the two warriors understood."

"But they didn't believe it! Nor you! So now you're on the warpath, raring to—"

"On the warpath, yes!" For once, an Indian committed the

discourtesy of interrupting a speaker in mid-sentence. Sakuruta had lived among white men for many years. "We did not believe Meserve, who told us your herd was going to Round Mountain. Meserve has Pawnee blood, but he is white and a government man!"

"He told you the truth!" Mike said.

"The two warriors heard you say that it was so, talking to him. That is why we are here, to look for you. We heard you sharpening the knife. Do you say to me you were taking your herd to Round Mountain?"

"Not mine. Cullen's herd."

"I believe you, Makegold!" said Sakuruta.

Mike was tempted to remark that it was damned big and white of him. "Meserve says you knew Cullen. I guess you know Hollinger, too."

"Where is Hollinger?"

"Down this creek with my herd and Cullen's herd in one bunch, and a crowd of scalawag Jayhawkers! I just came from there. Came looking for a gun. Care to loan me yours?"

Sakuruta dipped a glance at the clasp knife. "You would go back to fight them with that?"

Mike shrugged. "It's all I could find." He paused, and said, "See, Cullen's niece—they've got her."

His news didn't have the effect he thought it deserved. Sakuruta wasn't to be shaken by the fate of a mere woman, a white one at that. "Where is Meserve?" he asked.

"I'm afraid he's gone to stir up some horse soldiers," Mike told him, and a murmur passed through the band of warriors. Not, he thought, of fear. Of grim commitment, rather. "Look," he said to Sakuruta, "loan me a gun and a horse. If it's beef you're after, I'll take you to it! But any killing, I'll do it! Not you! Not any of your warriors!"

"I said we are on the warpath!" The chief stuck out his chin. "We are! Against Hollinger, who steals the beef meant for our people!"

"No scalp hunt! I won't go along with it! You kill Hollinger or anybody else, you're through! Meserve made that clear to me before he left. You'll have the army on your necks, and I'll be on the renegade list for riding in with you!"

Sakuruta snorted. "We ride to the enemy, but must not fight?"

"That's how it's got to be, Chief," Mike said. "You ride in for cattle. My business is at the house."

"How do we get the cattle without fighting? You talk like

a fool, Makegold!" A loud spit went with the comment, registering angry disgust. "We have guns! They will shoot at us, and we—"

"You'd make a battle of it!" Mike cut in. "Whichever way it came out, it would amount to the same thing—Pawnee war party attacked white men! That's how the Washington folks would see it. The rights and wrongs of it would get lost in the shuffle. You ought to know that."

"When is the Indian ever in the right?"

"Never, if he shoots a white man! Look at it straight, Chief. If you whipped the Hollinger bunch in a battle, then what? You couldn't drive the cattle up to Round Mountain, with the soldiers out after you. You'd have to fight them, too! Then the rest of your people, they'd pitch in. Meserve was right. It'd spread. We'd end up with a hell of a dirty war, like the one that got started by a Sioux who busted a white settler's grindstone. Don't call me a fool! You'd be the fool, condemned by all white men and cursed afterwards by your own people for leading them into destruction!"

It was a long speech for Mike, and all he got in return for it was a grunt. Sakuruta pulled his blanket about him, a sign that he had nothing more to say, his black glare proclaiming that he resented what had been said to him.

"I want your gun and shells, a horse, and your promise to hold your braves in line!" Mike said. "Or go your own way. I can't stop you from fighting Hollinger's Jayhawkers, but I've scouted the layout and I doubt you can make it."

Sakuruta took time to make up his mind. Logic evidently at last penetrated past his warlike temper, while he hated giving in to it. Glowering, he tossed his cartridge belt and holstered gun ungraciously at Mike's feet. He spoke to the warriors in guttural Pawnee.

They slipped off without a sound, reminding Mike that the name Pawnee, or Pá-ni, meant Wolf. He could only hope, not knowing their tongue, that Sakuruta had impressed upon them the command that they weren't going on a scalp-hunting expedition tonight. They came back mounted, one of them leading up a spare pony for Mike.

The Indian pony disliked his smell and sidled off, eyes rolling white, giving him some trouble to leg onto the saddle. He took the lead, saying, "We'll work something out as we go along, Chief."

He described in detail the terrain, the gap and the valley opening out beyond, the headquarters location, and made proposals as to how a pitched battle might be avoided. It was a monologue, none of the following Pawnees offering a word either of agreement or dissent.

Sakuruta didn't so much as grunt, never turned his head, disdaining to show by the slightest sign that he understood what Mike was saying. His bad temper erected a wall against the white man's tongue. He had gone blanket.

Mike stopped talking, finding that he was only repeating himself in a vain attempt to draw out some kind of response. The trouble with so many Indians, he reckoned, was that they blinded themselves to consequences. Like fatalists, they seemed to take the viewpoint that the future bore little relation to the present, still less to the past.

Here was Sakuruta, wise as he was, acting as bitterly sullen as an old colonel deprived of his command. Yet he knew, as well as anybody, that the white man's law was intolerant of any Indian attempt to redress wrongs by force. Let a battle flare up, the Pawnees would take all the blame. The habit of blaming the Indian was pretty deeply inplanted in the mind of officialdom. At the least, some prejudiced fool behind a desk hundreds of safe miles away would demand wholesale arrests. The army would march forth on orders to subdue the treacherous Redskins, and the guilt of Hollinger and his Jayhawkers would be lost in the smoke.

Mike wished Sakuruta would recognize that, and try being a good Indian without making of himself a dead one.

CHAPTER FIFTEEN

The gap was unguarded, a circumstance that could be interpreted two ways. The Jayhawkers were either supremely cocksure of the security of the Hollinger headquarters, or their spies had warned them of the coming invasion and they had prepared a trap farther on.

Mike hipped around in his saddle for a look back. In the moonless dark of the gap he couldn't tell how many of the Pawnee warriors still trooped behind him. Nor did he know how much of his talk Sakuruta had relayed to them, if any.

He pointed northward to the slopes overlooking the valley, for them to take that course, then swept his hand toward the lights of the ranch headquarters, high south. The lights were fewer. He reckoned the time at around three o'clock.

"I go there!"

Beside him, Sakuruta jerked his chin upward, Indian-like, the motion tantamount to a shrug, and spoke for the first time in a long spell. "How many there?"

"Not sure. Many, perhaps." Mike drew the gun that Sakuruta had thrown to him, and checked its loads. The gun was a Colt's Dragoon .44, Thuer-tooled for center-fire shells. He liked it, liked its hefty weight and balance, all six cylinders full. The Lord only knew where Sakuruta had got hold of such a good and dependable gun, a long sight better than the cap-and-ball pistols issued to the army. "I go there alone, Chief!"

"Go, fool!" growled Sakuruta, and added something in Pawnee, probably an insult too broad to be translated into English. The old man was still mad at him, angry over being

114

shunted into second place and made to promise not to shoot anybody.

"Remember, Chief, your warriors shoot in the air, or at the ground—anywhere but at a white man!" Mike gave him final reminder. "You've got to come out of this clean!"

Sakuruta turned away without responding. Mike looked doubtfully after him, wondering how deep was his anger and his sense of injured prestige, and how far he could be relied on to carry out his part in the raid. His ugly temper made him unpredictable. He was apt to look for a fight. Or follow an irate impulse to pull out of the valley and leave the offending Makegold holding the bag.

Putting aside his doubts and misgivings, Mike rode on alone until the lights of the Hollinger headquarters took on the shapes of three windows and an open door. That had to be as far as he dared ride. He needed the pony close in for a getaway, but it didn't step as soft-footed for him as it did for a Pawnee, seeming to take a perverse pleasure in kicking stones. He tied the animal to a hackberry shrub and went on foot, skirting a wide course around the buildings.

It cost time to make his roundabout approach, more time than he had figured on, which he feared would upset the schedule he had arranged with Sakuruta. Only the front room of the house was lighted, and he had spied no men in the yard. The rear of the house bulked black in the darkness.

He crept toward it, hurrying more than caution dictated, bearing in mind his schedule. At any moment now the first shots should ring out from the gap, by prearrangement creating a diversion, a dash to the spot by the Jayhawkers.

Few windows had been built into the back of the house, and those were small and high. He had no idea which room it was that Joyce occupied. How to find out stumped him. Tossing gravel at one window after another was asking for a gun welcome.

He crouched waiting for the shots in the gap. His worry mounted as the minutes passed, became racking anxiety. Indians in general gave small concern to clocked divisions of time, and an hour to them might cover anything from thirty minutes up to half a day, but that didn't apply to Sakuruta.

The night would soon be gone. Mike fingered gravel and looked up at each small window, wishing for a hunch to guide his choice. Sakuruta had pulled out, quit. . . .

A chatter of shots brought a start from him. He had given up hope of them. They rattled in the gap, and as suddenly

ceased. A dead silence stretched for seconds, then the ranch
erupted like a sleeping army fort attacked. The bunkhouses
reverberated, men stamping their boots on and piling out on
the run. They didn't waste much breath shouting questions.
These hardcase Jayhawkers lived on the edge of violence,
day and night. Their reactions were prompt, trimmed to es-
sentials.

Mike heard Keeley calling out, "Some of you drop down
the west end and cover it! Nev' mind getting horses—jump
to it! Them with horses handy, get there fast and block off
this end! The rest fan out and follow. Look for anybody's
got through!"

Hollinger's voice sounded, and Keeley answered, "No,
sir, but we'll sure find out! Yeah, 'bout a dozen shots. Car-
bines, I'd say, and maybe a six gun or two."

"Queer! Perhaps a couple of our men were coming in with
reports, and ran into strangers. Cavalry?"

"Sounded like a fast shoot-out, anyhow! They'll get a
faster one!"

"Make sure none get away!" Hollinger warned.

"My boys'll tend to that!" said Keeley. There came a brief
pause. "If you ain't looked in on the young woman lately,
Mr. Hollinger, maybe I better."

"No, you go take a look at Gould. Those shots might
mean he's got friends searching for him."

Their voices dropped, Keeley walking across the yard to
Hollinger at the open front door. Mike crept to the corner
of the house to hear better.

Keeley said, "I can't find the damn key! The grain shed's
padlocked all right, though. I checked. But the key—"

"I don't like that!" Hollinger snapped. "Somebody must
have it! Somebody's trying to cross me!"

"No, sir, there ain't a man here who'd do that to help
Gould. Kill him, yeah, any of 'em would—but why sneak
in and kill him tonight, when he's sure to die hard in the
morning? It'd be doing him a favor!"

"But those shots, and the key missing—"

"I only know of one who'd want to take that key, and it
ain't a man," Keeley said. "It's a woman! Yeah, her! Was
there any way she coulda got hold of it?"

"We'll find out! Come on in."

The light from the front room dimmed, and Mike heard
both men pace across the bare floorboards, one of them evidently carrying the lamp from the table. Three riders can-

tered into the yard and pulled up before the house. Mike drew back flat against the side wall.

One lighted lamp remained in the front room, and the three riders bent to peer in. Not seeing Hollinger or Keeley, only the empty room, they conferred together in mutters. Mike edged off to the rear of the house. A moving light glimmered on one of the small windows. He was straightening up to the window when the three riders came around the house at a walk, and silently cursing them he dropped to the ground.

They passed within fifty feet of him, still talking together, headed in the direction of the upper valley. After their backs were toward him and receding, he looked up at the window. It showed blank, not a glint of light behind it.

Inwardly raging, he went around to the front of the house at almost a sprint. There he slowed to tiptoe four long paces that brought him up close to the open door. Both lamps burned in the front room. A steady tapping sounded. Somewhere a horse's hoofs beat an approach. Keeley's voice reached him clearly.

"I think we're wasting time, Mr. Hollinger! You want me to search her?"

He moved to the edge of the door and looked in, while his ears registered the beat of the approaching horse; a ragged beat as of a horse lamed, but ridden regardless.

Hollinger sat drumming his fingernails on the table, staring at Joyce. The inquisitor and judge, he kept his protruding eyes fixed unblinkingly on hers. She stood before him as the prisoner at the bar. Behind her stood Keeley, as jailer.

Receiving no answer, Keeley asked again, "You want me to search her?"

Hollinger shook his head slightly, impatiently, without removing his eyes from Joyce. His fixed stare and monotonously drumming fingernails were aimed to break her down, reduce her to groveling confession by the force of his will. The fact that she merely stared back, giving not the slightest sign of groveling, didn't appear to disconcert him as yet.

Keeley let out a faint sigh, his eyes roving over her. "If she's got it I'll find it, guar'ntee you that!"

It brought a dark scowl from Hollinger. He broke his stare and exploded, "When I want her searched, I'll tell you! Go and see what they're doing at the gap!"

"Well, we don't hear any—"

"Go!"

Keeley shrugged sullenly. In the act of turning, he saw Mike standing at the open door, gun in hand. On the instant, he seized Joyce and swung her before him.

Starting to his feet, Hollinger barked at him, "What are you—!" Sudden awareness of Mike's presence choked him off. His mouth stayed open. His eyes bulged. For the moment his massive self-assurance deserted him and he remained half-risen from his chair, shaking his head slightly in disbelief.

The amazement then hit Keeley. His action had sprung from instinct at the sight of an intruder holding a pointed gun. It was the gun that impelled him in a flash to seize Joyce as the nearest shield, like a man throwing up his arm to ward off an unexpected blow. Now he narrowed a perplexed glare at Mike.

"Who the hell let you out?"

Hollinger was first to recover himself. He stood upright, rolling his shoulders as though donning a cloak of command, composing his heavy features, regaining his majestic bearings. "Yes, who?"

"It wouldn't profit you to know," Mike said. "Sit down!"

Hollinger's cheeks puffed angrily. "Do you think you can—"

"I can! Sit down!" Mike turned the gun on him, aimed at his thick middle, and Hollinger slowly sank into the chair. "Hands on the table and keep 'em there!"

He gave sharp attention to Keeley, wishing that Keeley's puzzled uncertainty could have lasted a bit longer. A keen combative urge had replaced it. The lariat master, defeated in his prideful field by a tie-fast, short-rope Texan, showed by his alert eyes the thirst in him to even the score. Mike took a pace forward into the room.

"Joyce, come here round me! Let go of her, Keeley!"

Keeley bent his knees quickly, bobbing down behind her, his hands grasping her arms. He pulled her close to him and whipped his left arm around her, freeing his right hand.

"Let your gun be!" Mike warned him.

Joyce made an attempt to break free. Keeley clutched her tighter to him, and she heeled him in the shins. He breathed curses. She made none too adequate cover for him, and her struggling and kicking kept him too occupied to snatch out his gun. "Go ahead an' shoot!" he challenged. "It's her you'll hit!"

"Better than what you Jayhawker scum planned for her!"

Circling partly around the room, Mike watched for the chance of a shot, but Keeley kept Joyce between them. He stopped at the table and touched the muzzle to Hollinger's ear. "Tell him to let go of her, or you get it!"

Hollinger flinched. "Let her go, Lew!" he exclaimed.

"He ain't gonna shoot!" Keeley said. "He's bluffin'!"

"Do as he says, Lew!"

"They'd hear it down in the gap, an' come a-runnin'! He knows it, don't worry! If he was gonna shoot, he woulda cut loose soon's he come to the door."

Hollinger appeared to find no comfort in the reflection that the shot that brought the men would be the shot that blew his brains out. "Don't you see he's got his gun in my ear?"

"Sure, but you'll see I'm right," Keeley drawled. "We got nothin' to worry about. It's a standoff till the boys come back!"

Mike thought of the approaching rider on the lamed horse, and of the three who had come to the house and ridden on, likely to return soon. He had taken up too much time here.

"They won't be back for quite a while," he said. "They'll be busy dodging cattle in the gap."

Hollinger drew his head away from the muzzle. "There are no cattle in the gap."

"There will be!" Mike promised. "All those you've got in the valley. I'm having 'em moved out."

"Liar!" Keeley jeered. "You'd want plenty o' damn tough riders for that job!"

"I've got 'em! Sixty or more, all born scrappers!"

"Those carbine shots!" Hollinger exclaimed, and a look of outrage spread over his face. "The Pawnees, you mean? I don't hear any of their mongrel-yelping!"

"You'll hear 'em start the run any minute now," Mike told him. "And your Jayhawkers better hit for the high spots in a hurry, or get about five thousand cows on their necks! This time they'll know firsthand what the wrong end of a stampede's like, for a change!"

"Renegade!" Hollinger rasped. "You've gone renegade all the way!" His outrage was genuine. He could see no side but his own, and on his side any crime was condoned, while all others he condemned. "A squatter-helping, Indian-loving, stinking renegade!"

"Coming from you," Mike commented, "I take that as praise! I wouldn't want the boss Jayhawker to like anything about me! Keeley, I'll give you three seconds to turn her loose!"

"If I don't?"

"I'll buffalo this critter cold, then I'm coming—" Mike broke off, hearing the crunch of a footstep outside.

Phin Starr clumped in carrying a saddle on his shoulder, speaking as he entered. Besides having to adjust his eyes to the light, the saddle blocked much of his view of the room. "Something's going on up the valley," he said. "Dunno what, but the cows're kinda bunchin' up." He eased the saddle off his shoulder. "I'da got here sooner, only my jughead went lame on me."

Sensing something amiss, he turned for a full look about the room, and froze. "Jeez!" he muttered.

Mike had to back-step fast to get him covered along with Hollinger and Keeley. His change of position placed him in a corner, which didn't please him. "Drop the saddle and sit on it!" he said.

Starr hesitated, holding the saddle chest-high. His thin lips pressed downward, increasing the sourness of his face, and he sent Keeley a bleak look. Keeley put hard pressure into his arm around Joyce. It brought a gasp from her. Mike switched his gaze to her, and Starr immediately heaved the saddle at him and dug at his holster.

Mike dodged, fired. The corner restricted him. His bullet scored the saddle and caromed off. As the saddle thumped beside him, he fired again and got Starr in the final motion of lining up his gun. But Starr, too much the Jayhawker to know better than to gamble his life on Keeley's mute message, had served his purpose.

CHAPTER SIXTEEN

Keeley fired around Joyce. Her constant struggling spoiled his aim, and on his second try she struck at his poking forearm. His gun went off, wasting a shot at the floor. Her heels rained back-kicks at his shins. She would not let up on him, would not give him one instant to steady his gun.

In a rage of exasperation, he raised the gun and brought the heel of the butt down on her head. She slumped small, head lolling, more of an encumbrance to him than a shield. He let her fall, and got off a shot while stepping over her.

Mike, his left arm bullet-ripped, blazed twice at him. To do it, he had to give Hollinger his chance. He saw Keeley stumble, pull up, then turn toward the doorway leading to the back rooms, walking in an oddly sedate manner as if he had lost all interest in the fight.

His elbow resting on the table, Hollinger was taking deliberate aim at him. In the close light of the table lamp his heavy face showed completely expressionless. He had taken off his hat, and his yellow hair glinted dully like tarnished brass. Mike dived to the floor, hastily slinging a wild shot to rattle his aim. He had one shell left in the Dragoon .44.

He heard running horses. Behind him, a hammer clicked to full cock. He rolled over. Keeley hadn't gone on through the rear door. He stood leaning against the wall beside it, using both hands to manipulate his gun. It was pointed at Joyce on the floor, either by malevolent design, or because he lacked the strength to raise it higher. His head was sinking forward while his finger pressed on the trigger.

The Dragoon .44 roared, and Keeley dropped. Mike slashed it around to bear on Hollinger.

"It's empty," Hollinger said matter-of-factly. "I counted your shots." He tapped the table with his gun. "Drop it and come here—on your knees!"

Three riders pounded into the yard, shouting Hollinger's name.

He said to Mike, "You lied about the Pawnees, didn't you? About running off my cattle? Answer me!"

"Not your cattle," Mike said. "Hers and mine."

"You lied!"

"If you want to think so, all right."

The horses stamped to halt outside. One of the riders called, "Mr. Hollinger! The cows are comin' down the valley!"

"What?" Hollinger jerked his head around. "You sure?"

"Yessir—whole damn lot of 'em's on the move! What was all the shootin' here?"

"Never mind that! Get on down to the gap and tell everybody to head them off! Tell them to throw a string of brush fires—"

Mike plunged into the table and upended it. Hollinger's cocked gun exploded a shell at the roof, Hollinger capsizing backward over his chair, the table on top of him. A puff of fire burst from the overturned lamp.

The table came pitching back at Mike, and Hollinger scrambled up, clawing at his burning, oil-soaked clothes. Flames enveloped him. He blundered to the door, a living pillar of fire, uttering frantic sounds, and rushed on out, making for the horse trough. The three horses reared back squealing in fright at the flaming apparition.

Mike scooped up Starr's fallen gun, and crawled to Joyce. She was slowly blinking her eyes, frowning while she tenderly touched the top of her head, unsure of what had happened. He listened to running hoofbeats, the slap of empty stirrups, to Hollinger's mouthings and men's tight-voiced cursing. A patch of spilled oil burned and fluttered out, leaving black-scorched floorboards. Hollinger must have caught most of the oil, the lamp falling on him. Mike lay watching the doors and windows, waiting for the three men to come at him.

A rising bedlam of noise swelled from the valley. It began with wild, high-pitched yells, Pawnee war cries, soon drowned out under the massive roar of five thousand bawling steers on the run. It hadn't suited the Pawnees to start the run from the upper end of the valley and give warning.

They had quietly eased the cattle onward before them into one huge gather, in the dark, and sprung the stampede on the last half-mile. The Jayhawkers in the gap would have to jump lively, especially those on foot.

"There they go!" Joyce mumbled.

"Yeah, there they go," Mike said. "And here we are! I guess old Sakuruta's left us to get out any way we can. I riled him pretty bad."

"Aren't there horses in the corrals here?"

"There are. And three soreheads waiting outside for us! I'd shoot out that other lamp if I thought it wouldn't set fire to the place. I'll see about it, when you can get around without falling over."

"I'm all right now," she said, "I think. Only a headache."

He paid her a quick glance. "You're still a mite sort of cross-eyed. Don't look too close at Kelley and Starr, or you'll have a relapse."

"You're trying to stir me up, aren't you?"

"That's about it."

Like prolonged thunder, the booming of the stampede rolled and echoed in the valley. He could tell when the cattle hit the gap, packed solid. It delayed them to funnel through. There'd be a few mangled carcasses left behind there. Be a wonder if they didn't widen the gap a bit, knocking off corners.

The racket muted, and he judged that the last of them had gone tearing through. The walls of the gap muffled their bawling, and then beyond the gap it fell to a growling murmur. He hoped Sakuruta's warriors could hold the cattle bunched, not let them break up and scatter. There were enough of them to handle it, if they all worked together.

He grew conscious of silence in and around the house. At the same time, Joyce murmured, "How quiet it is!"

Perhaps too quiet, he thought. The three men outside surely hadn't left. He held his breath, straining to listen, his eyes darting from doors to windows. His hand holding the gun grew sweaty. He thought he heard a slight rustle.

"Mike!" Joyce whispered. "Somebody's at the door!"

He trained his gun at the open door. A scarlet-tipped feather came poking into view. It waved coyly. He let his breath out in a gust, rising to his feet, helping Joyce up.

"How, Chief!" he said solemnly.

Sakuruta came stalking in, looking smug. "How, Make-gold!" He deigned to pay Joyce a lofty nod, superior male to mere female. Half a dozen of his warriors moved up to the door behind him. They eyed the bodies of Keeley and Starr unconcernedly, and Mike could guess why the three men outside were so quiet. Sakuruta looked suspiciously cheerful.

"You used my gun, Makegold? Good!" He picked it up off the floor. "This place has horses and saddles for you and your woman. We must catch up with the cattle. We must pass through the gap before light. Some enemies may be left there."

"Did Hollinger make it to the horse trough?" Mike asked him, walking to the door with Joyce. She stumbled against him.

"Your woman is weak," Sakuruta commented. "You must make her strong to bear children."

"She took a clout on her head."

"You should not beat a woman on her head, Makegold. It is her weakest part. The proper part of her to beat is—"

"The dark feller there did it," Mike told him. He repeated his question about Hollinger.

Sakuruta stared blankly at nothing. "His misery is ended."

The two herds traveled as one, beating northward up the last leg of the Round Mountain trail, sunlight flashing on warriors' red-tipped feathers and cavalrymen's brass buttons. As a trail outfit it was oversized and disorderly, a harum-scarum rabble. Four or five of the troopers, claiming they were ex-cowpunchers, had impressed on the Pawnees the need to hold positions on swing, flank and drag, but had a hard time restraining them from dashing up and down the column, putting on a grand show for the gaping benefit of the Hopewell settlers. They couldn't stop them from singing. The warriors sang interminably of victory over enemies.

"About as tuneful as a thousand tomcats!" remarked U. S. Marshal Meserve. "Guess I'm too white to 'preciate it."

He had found a nine-man patrol on the Fort Smith road and talked their young lieutenant into turning back with him. They hadn't come up to the herd until after Mike and the Pawnees swung it off the Baxter Springs trail and were approaching the Hopewell settlement. Meserve was being reticent, not yet mentioning from what point he had begun tracking the herd. Mike hoped he would refrain from asking too many awkward questions. Still, Meserve would have to know some facts, to put into his report. And the lieutenant as well.

The young lieutenant was torn between worry over having exceeded his routine patrol duty, and a too-obvious pleasure at meeting Joyce in doing so. Meserve assured him that he would take full responsibility and even put in a commendation to division headquarters; but his authority was civil, not military. He didn't have to face the ire of a stiff-necked post commander.

He said to Mike, "Sakuruta's sent word on to the Indian Agent to let him know we're coming."

Mike nodded, knowing it to be an opener to further talk on Meserve's part. "*Bueno*. He's told me." He and Joyce were riding side by side ahead of the herd. He wished Meserve and Sakuruta would drop back. The lieutenant, too. There they were, right up close behind.

He glanced aside at Joyce. "We've got to know each other pretty well now, eh? I mean, well enough so we get along."

She inclined her head gravely. "Pretty well."

He stared forward for a minute. "If the Indian Agent can't buy the whole lot for Round Mountain, I'll get some of these Hopewell folks to help me drive my cows on up to Arkansas City, and sell out there. Then I'll cut over to Abilene."

"What's in Abilene?"

"My Lost Creek crew. I'll round 'em up and see they get back home."

"That's most thoughtful of you," she said coolly. "I'm sure I can find a place in Hopewell to stay."

He shook his head. "No, I'd have to come back here to pick you up."

"Pick me up? Like supplies? By then I'll be on my way back to Colorado!"

"That's what I'm afraid of. So you come along with me."

"That sounds like an order!"

He turned to her, seeing her flushed face and blazing eyes. By God, she'd always be a handful. "Be good, now," he murmured, only for her to hear. "Sakuruta gave me ideas. He keeps a quirt for his women when they don't behave!"

"I'm not your woman!" she flashed.

He twisted from his little finger the silver ring that he had taken from Sakuruta in trade. This, he thought, was a hell of a way to do it, showing none of the tenderness that he felt for her. No privacy around a trail outfit. He reached to her left hand and slipped the ring over her finger.

"You are now! We'll be married in Arkansas City, or else Abilene. You be good!"

She closed her hand tightly. "Y-yes, Mike," she stammered, her color higher, her eyes melting. "I—I'll be good."

Mike figured it was just between them, unobserved by anyone else, but behind them Chief Sakuruta grunted approval, and wheeling his pony he rode back to his singing warriors. There would be a great feast and all-night dancing after the herd was delivered, the Pawnee women probably urging Joyce to consider a simple Indian wedding as eminently convenient and time-saving. The bewitched young lieutenant, equally observant, sighed heavily and dropped back to dwell on his worries.

Meserve, preoccupied with his problems, pushed his horse on abreast of Mike's. Discarding his careful reticence, now that the lieutenant was out of earshot, he said, "Gould, you pulled one over on me! Soon's I was gone, you went and got my Pawnees and took 'em on a raid against Hollinger!"

"It wasn't that way at all," Mike contradicted him. "They were set on going after the cattle. I went along to keep 'em out of mischief." He gave the marshal an account of what had happened, trimming it down somewhat. Joyce kept nodding corroboration and putting in a word now and then.

"You're a pair! How well did you keep 'em out of mischief?" Meserve's tone was skeptical. "I found Hollinger's layout. I scouted on ahead of the lieutenant, and turned him back before he saw it. Lucky I did! It was empty—plucked clean, and the house burned to the ground! How'd that happen?"

"I guess some of the Jayhawkers took what horses were left," Mike said. He had seen a glow in the rear, when coming out through the gap. While he and Joyce got horses from one of the corrals, Sakuruta and the half-dozen picked warriors with him had certainly had time to set fire to the house for good reasons of their own.

"Hum! Was there a fight? A shooting fight, I mean. I didn't find anybody dead there." Meserve squinted at Mike. "Of course, any dead bodies could've got dragged into the house before it burned, couldn't they?"

"Maybe somebody'll sift the ashes one of these days."

"For bones? A lot they'd prove!" Meserve rode in silence for a while, frowning thoughtfully. Finally he said, "I suspect you know Hollinger's never going to turn up alive! We'll know how to smash his system for selling stolen beef, if anybody else ever tries it. Selling stolen beef to the government itself, by damn!"

He wagged his head. "They won't try that again, not the Jayhawkers. With Hollinger out of it, they're done. Oh, we'll have 'em around, sure. Running in gangs, like they used to. They won't be organized, though. Won't have Hollinger's brains and money back of them. Nor his ranches."

"Nor his madness!" Mike put in.

"If that's what it was. No, the big day of the Jayhawkers is all over. I," Meserve stated calmly, "aim to take the credit for it! That is, if you don't compete for it."

"Not me! The credit might's well go to somebody it'll do some good."

"It won't do me good if it comes out the Pawnees jumped Hollinger and wiped him out! Hollinger was a big man, a white man, solid citizen. I took on to be responsible for these Pawnees."

"They had to do some shooting," Mike told him carefully, "but they didn't shoot anybody. They shot in the air, I give you my oath." He turned to Joyce. "That right, honey?"

"Right!" she seconded him promptly. "They're very good people, peaceful and respectable, and—and their attitude toward women is—is admirable!"

"Hum!" grunted Meserve, hearing such eulogizing of Pawnees for the first time in his life, and looking at her askance as if she had praised Satan and all his works. "All right, I'll report they behaved themselves and didn't shoot anybody. I notice, though, you don't say anything about knives, spears, clubs, or bare hands! And neither will I!" He reined off to drop back, and paused.

"But look!" he said, raising a knotty finger. "Sakuruta's got a fresh scalp at his belt, know that? It's a yellow one, singed at the ends, and he better keep it out of sight!"

L(eonard) L(ondon) Foreman was born in London, England in 1901. He served in the British army during the Great War, prior to his emigration to the United States. He became an itinerant, holding a series of odd jobs in the western States as he traveled. He began his writing career by introducing his most widely known and best-loved character, Preacher Devlin, in "Noose Fodder" in *Western Aces* (12/34), a pulp magazine. Throughout the mid thirties, this character, a combination gunfighter, gambler, and philosopher, appeared regularly in *Western Aces*. Near the end of the decade, Foreman's Western stories began appearing in Street & Smith's *Western Story Magazine*, where the pay was better. Foreman's first Western novels began appearing in the 1940s, largely historical Westerns such as *Don Desperado* (1941) and *The Renegade* (1942). The *New York Herald Tribune* reviewer commented on *Don Desperado* that "admirers of the late beloved Dane Coolidge better take a look at this. It has that same all-wool-and-a-yard-wide quality." Foreman continued to write prolifically for the magazine market as long as it lasted, before specializing exclusively for the book trade with one of his finest novels, *Arrow in the Dust* (1954) which was filmed under this title the same year. Two years earlier *The Renegade* was filmed as *The Savage* (Paramount, 1952), the two are among several films based on his work. Foreman's last years were spent living in the state of Oregon. Perhaps his most popular character after Preacher Devlin was Rogue Bishop, appearing in a series of novels published by Doubleday in the 1960s. George Walsh, writing in *Twentieth Century Western Writers*, said of Foreman: "His novels have a sense of authority because he does not deal in simple characters or simple answers." In fact, most of his fiction is not centered on a confrontation between good and evil, but rather on his characters and the changes they undergo. His female characters, above all, are memorably drawn and central to his stories.